REINHARDT'S
GARDEN

REINHARDT'S GARDEN

Mark Haber

COFFEE HOUSE PRESS
Minneapolis
2019

Coffee House Press books are available to the trade through our primary distributor, Consortium Book Sales & Distribution, cbsd.com or (800) 283-3572. For personal orders, catalogs, or other information, write to info@coffeehousepress.org.

Coffee House Press is a nonprofit literary publishing house. Support from private foundations, corporate giving programs, government programs, and generous individuals helps make the publication of our books possible. We gratefully acknowledge their support in detail in the back of this book.

LIBRARY OF CONGRESS CATALOGING-IN-PUBLICATION DATA

Names: Haber, Mark, 1972–author.
Title: Reinhardt's garden / Mark Haber.
Description: Minneapolis : Coffee House Press, [2019]
Identifiers: LCCN 2018053577 (print) | LCCN 2018055655 (ebook) |
    ISBN 9781566895705 (ebook) | ISBN 9781566895620 (trade paper)
Classification: LCC PS3608.A23835 (ebook) | LCC PS3608.A23835
    R45 2019 (print) | DDC 813/.6—dc23
LC record available at https://lccn.loc.gov/2018053577

PRINTED IN THE UNITED STATES OF AMERICA

26 25 24 23 22 21 20 19   1 2 3 4 5 6 7 8

To Ülrika

"A most incomparable delight it is so to melancholize, and build castles in the air, to go smiling to themselves, acting an infinite variety of parts, which they suppose and strongly imagine they represent, or that they see acted or done."

—Robert Burton, *The Anatomy of Melancholy*

"The ill humor, or despondency, that characterizes a melancholic is not merely an endurance, a lethargic toleration, of existence, but an *active re-creation* of it: melancholics live in the same world as other people, yet they do not see the same world. They build for themselves a new world into which they alone can enter." —László F. Földényi, *Melancholy*

"He was standing on it, had been treading its surface all along, and was fated to proceed along it in the immediate future, and as he noted this, he put his belated recognition of it down to the fact that it was all too obvious, too close, and its unsuspected proximity was the problem; it was because he could touch it, indeed walk all over it, that he had ignored it."

—László Krasznahorkai,
The Melancholy of Resistance

REINHARDT'S
GARDEN

1907

The Río de la Plata is a corpulent snake, mused Ulrich; it nestles around your neck, it strangles you for your wallet or wedding band, anything of value, he said; whoever escapes alive? Ulrich said this to no one, not expecting a reply, at least not from me, since I could hardly understand a word he said, my brain coated in the gauze of the fever or disease or whatever it was I'd been afflicted with, and I was certain I was dying, I had to be dying, because the tremors, the aches, my burning flesh, none of it boded well for recovery. Inherently Ulrich understood this, and I suspected he was talking to me out of camaraderie, sensing my advance toward the land of the dead, and being a sensitive type beneath it all, he wanted to give my soul the solace of another voice. Already we'd buried ten men, native guides as well as whites, but this wasn't a typical malady; I felt the universe inside my skull, felt the shifting latitudes of the world as it trembled through space. And not five feet away sat Jacov, oblivious, licking the nub of a pencil, scribbling in his notebook, busy with his treatise on melancholy, his life's work, claiming only yesterday that he was closer than he'd ever been, closer to the essence of melancholy, the foundation of melancholy, the seed of melancholy, assuring anyone who would listen that he would be the first important name to emerge from Knin, that village that lay crouched in the Dalmatian hinterland like a frightened child. Jacov, who not three days earlier had insisted he'd seen it with his own eyes. Melancholy? I'd inquired. No, you imbecile, the source. And after smoking a glut of cigarettes, he proceeded to measure the base of a rubber tree where five Indians sat listlessly on their haunches awaiting instructions. They'd begun to suspect Jacov of madness weeks before when he'd ordered three Guaraní Indians to circle the camp as we slept, one clockwise, two counter. The Guaraní hated him especially and had stopped attempting to hide it, letting their displeasure be known in subtle but intentional acts: misplacing gun powder or jerky or dry socks, dipping the tips of their poisoned spears in water, thus diluting them and making them less effective, even halting the mules the moment we made any progress. To Jacov, who suspected treason everywhere, this only confirmed his suspicions. Half delirious, I considered Jacov and his life's work, which had found me tramping behind him for the latter half of my youth, eleven years if I counted correctly; eleven years of taking dictation, eleven years of nodding agreement with ideas beyond the scope of my comprehension, from Croatia to Hungary, Germany to Russia, and now the Americas, lost in the lower groin of this hateful jungle. I cursed Jacov's perfect health, something he would boast about when any of us, including the natives, showed the slightest hint of an ailment: a cough in the hand, a twitching eye, a complaining stomach; Jacov pounced on this, perhaps searched for it, not only to parade his perfect constitution (showing a lack of common decency and ruthless self-pride) but also to celebrate the outstanding condition of his own body, thus mocking the burden others faced with their everyday infirmities. People are weak and filled with treachery, he lamented, a vomitous lot, an abhorrent lot; then, intoxicated by his own vitriol, he scanned the brows of the present assemblage: Mestizo, Guaraní, and more than a few of indeterminate origin. And me, he concluded, pointing sadly at himself, I must count myself among them. He abhorred society as well as the individual and took great pains to make his stance known, yet Jacov had made melancholy his life's work, striving to help a species he detested largely due to the unsung depths of his soul, insisting his desire to improve his fellow man was simply a reflection of his own character, what he likened to a *wellspring of benevolence.* Back in Stuttgart, where I'd officially begun to serve as his factotum, he would rant about the sick joke of human progress. Humanity and their delusions, he complained, people and their notions of enlightenment; well, Yasnaya Polyana has certainly cured me of that! Indeed it had. After Russia and that shameful mess with Tolstoy and his followers, it was clear Jacov would have to go his own way. What was there to do but change continents, he concluded, exchange Europe for the Americas? Let's go see the jungle, he proclaimed, sniffing a line of cocaine from a tray placed precariously on the arm of his settee. Europe is a graveyard, he said, a plot of black earth, a field of dead ends and bad endings and no-turning-backs, he intoned. Besides, we must find Emiliano Gomez Carrasquilla, the lost philosopher of melancholy who resides, I last heard, in the jungles of Colombia or perhaps Brazil, in any event, the Americas, all this spoken with the nonchalance of a madman, as if the Americas were the suburb of some middling city. Yes, he urged, looking into my now-trembling eyes, melancholia is to be found in the shrewd words of Emiliano Gomez Carrasquilla, in his divine works and sacred texts, his philosophic essays, and, of course, in speaking to him in person, beholding him in the flesh, considering the certitude of his beliefs face-to-face and most certainly not in the mediocrity of this continent. Let's see the jungle, where, I suspect, melancholy, like the vines themselves, runs verdant and slapdash across the landscape. Inside I laughed, for Europe, I felt, was the birthplace of melancholy or, if not the birthplace, at least the place where melancholy was perfected, where melancholy flourished, where melancholy found the most agency and thus became more vigorous and substantial; who else could lay claim to the saddest, most endless winters? Where but Europe was characterized by vast landscapes punctuated by graves, imbued by a desolation matched only by the most maudlin skies in the world? And why did my anxiety rise whenever Jacov snorted his beloved cocaine? Why did the drug affect me as if by osmosis? And I trembled at the enormous still lifes across his walls, the Goya towering in the adjoining room, the only painting, he claimed, that ever approached the turmoil of his soul. I then gazed at four paintings that had captivated me ever since Jacov acquired them on a trip to Holland, paintings that lured my unconscious with their thick streaks of lustrous blue and stark red: a series titled *Trembling of the Soul,* soldiers depicted in a barren field up to their knees in snow, the men symbolizing agents of death or perhaps the brevity of life or maybe the yawning chasm of an existence devoid of meaning, Jacov wasn't sure, but all four paintings spoke to one another and only succeeded, in fact, when placed together, as useless separated, he insisted, as a man's top half would be were it separated from his lower. Jacov was so enraptured he purchased the entire series, as well as a triptych of naked Romanian gypsies, all packed and sent to his castle in Stuttgart, occupied in his absence by one-legged Sonja, a retired prostitute, an ex-lover of Jacov's, and an invaluable housekeeper, the only person, in fact, he trusted enough to care for his estate since Jacov demanded all sorts of eccentric cleaning routines based in large part on his desire for seclusion, his paranoia to germs, and his obsession with dust, not its eradication, but its preservation, dust being emblematic of melancholy and the harbinger perhaps of a deeper, more divine melancholy that would be closer to reaching the pure path of unfettered melancholy, which would be akin to finding a new planet. Jacov worshipped dust, he once confessed; I stand at the altar of dust, he said; dust is not only divine, he affirmed, it's more important than the soil itself. Jacov could expound for hours on dust: how dust is the most significant element in the universe, not millions of isolated particles, like most believe, but something wholly of itself, as singular and unified as fog. A home laden with dust, he explained, invites melancholy at its leisure; it doesn't insist or make demands but beckons, he said, and the soul is encouraged to reflect on darker, more substantial notions since the dust, in a window, for example, creates a film that distorts the natural world. Just as melancholy darkens one's worldview, he continued, not to alter reality but to transpose reality, to elevate reality, to *improve* reality, dust does the same. All those philosophical imposters, as Jacov called them, those vulgar and insignificant nonentities, he stewed, who consider melancholy an affliction of the soul, those same shallow cretins also see dust as an affliction; they demand it be swept up, eradicated, forgotten. Defending himself from imagined slights, Jacov paced the study and tugged at his smock; why wouldn't I examine something as miraculous as dust, he pondered, something that returns as soon as you've gotten rid of it, which, of course, you haven't since nothing could be more perverse, nothing more idiotic, nothing more revolting than the belief you've eradicated dust. Nothing is as dogged, in fact, as unimpeachable, in fact, as thoroughly ubiquitous, in fact, as dust. Dust and melancholy. And thus, Jacov spent a considerable amount of time studying the relationship between dust and melancholy and then melancholy and dust, over two years in fact, where dust was studied for weeks at a time and then melancholia. The third chapter of his treatise was dedicated to dust, examining how the melancholic spirit, though appearing fragile, was as vigorous as the particles we breathe and incur and invite inside our lives. I, of course, hadn't read that chapter, just as I hadn't read a single typed page of the masterwork he had me transcribe, mostly because he hadn't begun to type his monument to melancholy, being, as he liked to say, in the fomenting stage or the fostering stage or, if he was feeling especially frivolous, the *seducing* stage, although I was certain, when complete, his work would change the world, for I had observed Jacov scribbling in those notebooks for years, an expression of religious fervor traced across his pale, balding skull, too exultant, too radiant, too ecstatic not to be appreciated as a man with the highest erudition and not unlike a famous sculpture I'd once been shown of Seneca, whose existence I would've been wholly ignorant of had Jacov not relished comparing himself to the ancient seer. For more than a decade I'd transcribed the words of a man of the highest intellectual order, a man who, with an almost saintly calling, berated and exclaimed and expounded the most original and subtle ideas on that most elusive of emotions: melancholy, not a feeling but a mood, not a color but a shade, not depression but not happiness either, an enigmatic realm without inscription because, as Jacov put it, it was too glorious. Its relegation to a half feeling, a bastard feeling, a diluted feeling, was the root of Jacov's exasperation. Melancholy, he once told me in the gravest of tones, is the single most important thing in the world; none of us realizes it, but melancholy is the engine of human progress. His notebooks had grown in number, of course, from a single shelf to a wall to a venerable library that required outside storage that Jacov obtained with Ulrich's help, Ulrich knowing all sorts of people in the German underworld, lawful and criminal alike, and since Ulrich had a particular affection for estate ownership and the act of proprietorship, which, he frequently asserted, was the only asset a man could trust, procuring different properties for the safekeeping of Jacov's masterwork, at least for Ulrich, was child's play. Before leaving for South America, Jacov had spent weeks separating his journals to store them in countless vacant apartments and depots throughout Berlin, Salzburg, and even the Stuttgart estate, where Sonja with her one leg would protect them as she hobbled about collecting the dust; this system would not only keep his work from the hands of jealous scholars, he believed, but it would also make it more difficult, were they found, to piece them together. The most important books, the nucleus of his studies, the *Origin Books*, as he called them, stayed on his person at all times; these were the dictations I had made since becoming his secretary, abridged of course, but the essence of his masterwork; thus, two weeks later, once his works had been separated and locked away in various cities, Warsaw, Odessa, and Berlin among them, our travel arrangements to Montevideo were secured aboard the *SS Unerschrocken*, a voyage that introduced me to a world of torment and misery no human, I feel, has ever faced. There is seasickness and then there is the border of death, the indiscernible line the optimistic cling to and the suicidal yearn to cross. Fatigued by life, the elderly see this boundary and welcome it; to me it appeared as the lurching horizon of the Atlantic, rising up and down like the designs of a lunatic, unfettered and deranged, an ocean that demanded I vomit my soul across a third of the planet, a feeling I thought I had escaped until this cursed fever announced itself, first with chills, then with panic, and finally with difficulty breathing; now, lying on the floor of the jungle, I hear Jacov cursing at the guides to put me onto the stretcher, for we were heading back to Montevideo, not as a retreat, mind you, not as a withdrawal, he insisted, merely an opportunity to acquire medicine, as the natives don't frighten me and never have. We shall return to Montevideo, he demanded, not to escape impending attack, which, as some of you have implied, is all but assured, but to assuage the symptoms of my assistant. I felt no solace in this, for our landing in the city was not unlike observing your own reflection in the mirror after surviving a violent accident; it was a city of sorts, with all the familiar hallmarks indicative of a place where people decide, likely from exasperation or surrender, to simply stop, but with the shanties at the harbor, the vulgar and chaotic Spanish that seemed not spoken but bellowed, the low crop of hillocks in the foggy distance, even the ships floating atop the brown, murky water, it was, as Jacov exclaimed, a provincial shithole, a sweaty horse's ass. Not the ass of a prized horse or a half-decent horse or even the ass of a horse that could plow the fields with any regularity; no, it was the ass of a decrepit and mediocre horse, the ass of a horse seconds from being put down. The captain of the ship, an Uruguayan, overheard these remarks and took offense. Forgive me, Jacov replied, but shall we compare the city we left, Bremen, a romantic city, a historical city, a city with *breadth*, to this? You were with us as we departed, correct? You saw what I saw and this, Jacov now sweeping his hand across the horizon, how do you explain *this*? I gazed at the meager huts, the abysmal plazas clustered together like children on their first day of school, nervous and ill-prepared. Things didn't improve on land. Álvaro Diego Astillero, the officer assigned to assist us in hiring native guides, translators, and mules for our journey, was sweating through his uniform, although, admittedly, his grasp of German was impressive. He greeted us on the patio of a wooden structure that was covered in mosquito netting, a necessary precaution, he explained, due to a recent outbreak of dengue fever, although, he quickly assured us, it's nothing to be too concerned about. After offering us drinks of maté, he inquired about our field of study. Plants? He asked. Geography? He enjoined. The Indians? We shook our heads to all three. Melancholy, answered Jacov, spitting on the floor. Álvaro, a man in his early thirties with inkblack hair smoothed back with either pomade or sweat, was worried by this answer. It is, as Jacov has constantly proven, a frightening word, an off-putting word, a word ill at ease amid the rest of a sentence. Melancholy, which doesn't say anything but hints at everything, trenchant enough to make the greatest of men, Jacov for example, abandon all sorts of sundry life choices to dedicate their souls to the study and understanding and perhaps, when all is said and done, the grasping of this singular anguish. A person stricken with melancholy isn't stricken by grief or depression, Jacov often mused, feelings that emerge from concrete and palpable incidents like the loss of a limb or loved one, or a long, hard-fought illness. No, he insisted, melancholy is a state of mind tied inexorably to a person's capricious nature; as such, all the great artists and philosophers and musicians, in fact, the greatest historical examples, like his beloved Wagner, have suffered, withstood, and thus grown stronger and more singular from melancholia. A melancholic, at least inwardly, doesn't love his own brooding nature, Jacov insisted, but must accept it as one accepts having red hair or a cleft palate. Álvaro, sweat escaping his khaki uniform, understood this on some level, for he looked past the mosquito netting and sighed. Was he, Jacov queried, perhaps a melancholic himself? Álvaro either didn't understand the question or wanted to change the subject, trying to sell us on the delights of Montevideo, the charming taverns and the evening cockfights. Jacov was skeptical and I was useless, still tilting from ninety days at sea, ninety days that rattled my soul to its core; never before had my equilibrium been so perfectly banished; it was as though I were standing atop an ever-rotating globe, and

I couldn't get it to stop. Pitching across the Atlantic, I felt as if I was heaving toward my annihilation. Jacov often joined me in my cabin as I beseeched God to finish his work and take me, to release me from this mortal coil, which merely made Jacov laugh, hovering above as if he were performing an exorcism, insisting I go farther, insisting I was closer than I'd ever been to pure melancholy, insisting the pinnacle, the crown, the mantle of melancholy, was mine for the taking. As the ship plunged and the world listed, Jacov insisted I was a prisoner of my own soul, that my fear of suffering was irrational; I must, he said, grieve the younger years that were now behind me and accept the misery of existence. I vomited instead. Luckily, since stepping onto land, I'd felt the earth slow by half, and now all of us took turns silently peering through the netting. The dusty streets promised very little, and Jacov, looking impatient, his *Origin Books* bulging beneath his vest, inquired as to Ulrich's whereabouts. At the quay with our trunks, I told him. Jacov clicked his tongue and Álvaro, sweating more profusely, gazing uneasily at Jacov's hunched composure, suggested it wise we bring a priest into the interior, which was met with a cackle from Jacov. For what? Jacov asked. We don't need a priest nor God, so long as I have these, he said, scratching his vest where the *Origin Books* lay sequestered like ancient scrolls, and, taking a more active interest in Álvaro, Jacov suddenly pressed him on his ancestral and national makeup. Uruguayan? he asked. Argentine? I see your eyes are green, ancestors from

Europe, perhaps? A little Dutch or English in you? Again Álvaro
looked confused, perhaps offended, for it was likely unusual,
indeed rude, to ask a man you've just met about lineage, but to
Jacov, this was all that mattered, and it formed the foundation
of some of his most important decisions. I, for example, was his
right-hand man and Ulrich his left not due to any extraordinary talents on either of our parts but because Jacov had trouble
trusting a German like Ulrich as much as a fellow Croatian like
myself; my innate understanding of melancholy, he asserted,
though unspoken and reticent, was deeper and more profound than a German's, since a German's melancholy existed
within the confines of a German mind and a German heart,
which all belonged, of course, to a German soul. A German,
Jacov claimed, has the constant desire to overcome his melancholy or confront his melancholy or, at some level, *devour* his
melancholy, which is nonsense and ridiculous and why Germans
will never fully accept the breadth of a melancholic soul. A
Hungarian is the next best melancholic after a Croatian, he
would famously say, for we all know there is no one on earth
next to a Croat who understands or intuits or grasps melancholy more than a Hungarian, yet a Croatian remains superior
since a Croat contains melancholy not only in their heart but in
the very fiber of their being, and even at their happiest, most
celebratory occasions, a Croat will halt, slapped and muted by
their melancholic nature, by the sudden reminder that all is
futile, and living with a conscience constitutes a merciless

barrier to happiness, which is, of course, the pervasive and unassailable wall of existence, and though a Hungarian is very close to a Croatian, the Hungarian remains a notch or two lower, for I have seen, Jacov contended, perfectly miserable Hungarians lose themselves at baptisms and weddings, even celebrating the victories of their favorite football clubs, whichever preposterous club it may be, yes, suddenly forgetting themselves and the miserable lot that is life and genuinely enjoying themselves, and in the end, this disqualifies them entirely. Bosnians are prudent melancholics, he offered, practicing melancholics, he added, responsible melancholics, he concluded, but not even close to the second-place Hungarian melancholic, who, at twilight, when the diminutive light struck their brow at the most auspicious angle, was one of the most beautiful visions Jacov had ever witnessed. A Jewish melancholy was a subject all its own, he stated, and something he refused to examine, for a Jew's suffering was a schism, a crevasse, an endless riddle he would only consider navigating once his experiences had matured. A Russian was a downright brilliant melancholic but was in love with his own melancholia so that it was sentimental and embarrassing for anyone to witness and became pure theater, practically a pantomime of real melancholy since pure, unmolested melancholy doesn't produce tears or exhibit theatrics, and it certainly doesn't make demands on another. Melancholy, he professed, is a hymn, a falling leaf, a frozen stream in the still dead of winter. Melancholy is the song of the nightingale and the wordless harmony of a meadow, he said, now clutching his chest. These sentiments, spoken in rapid and fervent German, which Álvaro certainly couldn't grasp, resembled the same words I'd heard on first meeting Jacov eleven years earlier. I recalled his deep, resonant voice trembling across the upper deck of the Holstooraf Sanatorium and Spa, where I'd been sequestered for a course of treatment for my lungs, the upper deck where so many came to bathe and delight in the warm August sun suspended in the afternoon as if supplicated by the clusters of pale, plump tourists. I climbed the wooden stairs in search of that very sun only to hear the Croatian accent so familiar to my ears, an accent lambasting all those pseudo-melancholies that crammed the spa, all those mealy melancholies, he barked, those counterfeit melancholies, he cried, swarming like fat eels. To him it was nauseating. I'm nauseated, he said, observing you *taking a cure*, rippling in your bathing suits with no shame, with no sense of decency or respect for those around you, bathing suits, he later said, that exposed the mediocrities they were, for how could a soul grapple with their melancholic nature while rubbing oils all over their overfed bodies, bodies, he indicated, that contained melancholies far weaker and less notable than his. Duller too, and, quite frankly, he said, less heroic and spiritual than his own distinguished sadness. Abhorrent melancholies, he shouted, heinous melancholies, he barked, egregious melancholies that sullied his truer and more virtuous melancholy, his *holiest of all* melancholies, downright ruining the authentic melancholy that had followed him since his pale, sorrowful youth in that cold pit of a home with harsh and unloving parents and a sickly sister, a twin no less, a faithful consort, the only one who fathomed the full dimensions of Jacov's soul, a twin he helped nourish as best he could until she expired, adding a sheen, a brilliance, a luster to his own melancholia as he spent the next five years devising ways to escape Knin, that horrible stain, that embarrassment to Croatia and all of Europe, an eternal black mark on his once-immaculate soul that even after he'd escaped all those years ago, not a morning went by where Jacov didn't awaken to feel he had returned to the same place, or rather, that he'd never left. He was cursing at the sunbathers, cataloging his grievances, when his eyes landed on me. I had just arrived, wholly ignorant of what had triggered the outburst, and observing his face, the blue eyes trembling and which possessed an almost carnal mania, I couldn't understand what I was looking at, for I was young and inexperienced and hadn't yet seen much of the world and, collectively, humans struck me as a rather tranquil species. At the time Jacov hadn't yet lost all his hair, but the sides were all aflame, wispy blond with streaks of fiery orange; he resembled an angry clown whose makeup had melted or been washed away by inclement weather, or perhaps a clown who for years had been unemployed but played the part out of loyalty or stubbornness. He overheard me asking the attendant for a towel and immediately recognized my Dalmatian accent, an accent, he later explained, forever drenched in the inexplicable sadness indigenous to the region, a sadness singular and inimitable and attained only by a life spent in Croatia, with its peasant huts, its poor diet, its rocky cliffs, and, of course, those perverse hills that bestowed a native with a perpetual sense of dislocation, a dizziness that, to his mind, had no known cure. A fellow Croat! he shouted in a tone that couldn't be confused with anything but an insult to the French and German and Romanian tourists enjoying the sun, who took a cure at the Holstooraf Sanatorium and Spa to savor its lavish views and fastidious accommodations, as well as the interminable sunsets that lent even the coldest of souls a sense of nostalgia. Jacov insisted I take the chair beside him, and thus our bond began. This was also where Jacov met Sonja, recently retired from whoring; a Jewess working as a server at Holstooraf at the time, still with both legs intact, years away from losing one and thus gaining that gimp that was instantly recognizable as it thumped throughout Jacov's Stuttgart property, the cadence and weight communicating the degree of her bad mood, not to mention the quirk, both clever and disturbing, of striking a match across her wooden leg to light her Dutch cigarettes. Jacov inquired about the region of Croatia from which I hailed as well as what affliction I suffered. Do you expect to survive or die here? Survive, I answered timidly, mostly because I was young and possessed a downy coat of optimism across my virgin soul, and, to be frank, I wasn't very ill, but the diagnosis of tuberculosis that had almost formed on the doctor's lips, that had almost escaped from the doctor's mouth, that I'd almost heard him say aloud, was enough to send me galloping home and promptly packing my trunk. The mere anticipation of a diagnosis of TB and off I went, for I may not have been particularly unwell, but I wasn't exactly well either, and perhaps, as my stepfather implied, I was a measly neurotic, but he wasn't a doctor, simply a frustrated and unhappy cheesemaker, and who's to say what illness was and what it wasn't? Ultimately it was diagnosed as a weak strain of bronchitis, but this was discovered only later, after my fate had been sealed, that is to say, after my visit to Holstooraf and my introduction to Jacov and his rants and insults, which I'd never before seen anything resemble, with spittle ejected and eyes like unruly marbles, and so my destiny was determined as Jacov cursed the wretched and false melancholies that surrounded us, repellent melancholies that strangled and depressed him and pushed his own melancholy further away. Their false melancholy, he said, forces my authentic melancholy to obscure itself, to scurry away and mask itself. I thought the absence of melancholy was a thing to aspire to, I said, suggesting a life in search of happiness seemed the acme of a life well lived; Jacov couldn't contain his laughter, which resembled the sound of small, inscrutable bats fluttering off the Holstooraf deck toward the ever-darkening cliffs. This, he said, as well as other things he'd already observed, confirmed how little I knew. Melancholy, he asserted, the unspoken and spiritual sadness of the soul, is transcendental, divine, and nothing a wise person should run from, but instead something to meet head on, to aspire to. A perfect life, he said, a life fulfilled, a life of radiant splendor, he added, was a life lived in constant melancholy, and here, he bristled, gesturing at the portly tourists, healthy and sick alike, were souls in constant *retreat* from melancholy, in constant *escape* from melancholy, meaning, in other words, souls in the constant *pursuit* of happiness, which, he concluded, was as foolish as trying to pursue or escape your own destiny, a destiny that found me eleven years later tipping Álvaro Diego Astillero with German currency, which he politely refused, and Jacov, shifting the *Origin Books* once again, for they irritated his belly, inquiring about the second order of business, which was, of course, cocaine and was it readily available in Montevideo? The amount he'd ingested while crossing the Atlantic had greatly diminished his supply. The drug was, in many ways, the source of our first crisis in the interior, for it was Jacov's ruthless desire for the powder that aggravated our skirmish with the Yaro Indians mere weeks into our trek. Jacov hadn't secured enough of the drug in Montevideo, and we found ourselves, within a very short period, dealing with an extremely choleric Jacov, a Jacov listless and despondent, a Jacov irascible one moment, taciturn the next, unwilling to trek or talk, irritated by the trees, the damp air, the polyphonic chorus of equatorial noises advancing from all sides, sounds the primitives might've considered a symphony but to our European ears was petulant and grating and a violation of good taste. We hadn't yet accustomed ourselves to the forest, and Jacov's resonant voice, as always, spoke for me and Ulrich. This vile jungle, he fumed, this monstrous jungle, he cursed, this inscrutable jungle and its offensive and nauseating impenetrability! His mood made him impossible to approach, vacillating between sullenness and rage; the trees and mud, the mist suspended at eye level; existence itself became ill fitting. The threat of exhausting his cocaine loomed before Jacov's eyes like approaching doom. Often he would halt midstep, forcing the entire party to stop, simply to inspect the remaining sacks, obsessed over their diminished size and, as if to further torture himself with an act of self-sabotage, sniff more of the powder. The Yaro accosted our camp early in the morning; it was Ulrich who spotted them first. An early riser, Ulrich had been awake for hours, rolling cigarettes on the stump of a tree and pondering things as he was wont to do, eyes glazed over, his ample body situated in a position of acute concentration as if contemplating the nature of existence, a man of few words but great depth, depths I'd never seen firsthand but Jacov assured me existed, and in the end it was Ulrich's kindness as well as our mutual loyalty to our master that formed the nexus of our bond. Ulrich had two sidearms, which he fired into the air to alert the camp, causing confusion and sending three guides running into the forest not to be seen again. A Yaro issued a single arrow that at first appeared rather senseless, arcing across the lone patch of open sky, seemingly hanging in the air for a full minute before drifting innocently down and going straight into the thigh of a young guide, nothing very serious, but for souls like ours, unaccustomed to violence, it was a harrowing sight. Yet Ulrich remained calm, Ulrich, whose past had always been a vague sketch of nebulous shapes, and he handled himself with great poise, for one perceived instantly on meeting Ulrich, with his lantern jaw and the abstract symmetry of his generous forehead, not to mention the accompanying four-inch scar that foretold *this, this right here* was a dangerous man, *this* was a man not to be trifled with or challenged, for Ulrich wasn't merely formidable but intelligent too, and when he stood, it seemed an act with surplus stages, as if he were extending his body where a normal person, a *reasonable* person, would've already finished. In any event, six or seven Yaro approached with spears at the ready, a plethora of vibrant feathers covering their skulls as well as piercings and face paintings both elaborate and chilling. Through a series of gestures and blunt noises Ulrich was able to calm the attackers, though the Guaraní, our guides, had a long-standing feud with the Yaro over a trade involving sugar cane or soybeans, or maybe it was rice, and one of the two tribes, I don't know which, felt cheated, although it may have been the marriage of a chief's daughter and her dowry that had caused the discord, no one was certain; however, providence, so rare and inscrutable, smiled down upon us because the spears were lowered, and tensions eased. Ask them if they have cocaine, urged Jacov, not the least curious about the bad blood between the Yaro and the Guaraní, which had turned the jungle air thick with resentment, for the focus Jacov brought to his life's work he brought equally to cocaine, and the current need to consume the powder superseded the desire for anything else, and when Jacov became this way, his meditations on melancholy, his love for melancholy, his fervor about melancholy vanished entirely. Luckily, the Yaro had great quantities of cocaine, although in a different form, and they rarely used it, except for religious ceremonies or to celebrate the death of a bad god, I think, although they may have used the cocaine for medicine and funeral rites; it was all mystifying, due in large part to our interpreter, Javier, a Spaniard highly recommended by Álvaro Diego Astillero for his knowledge of local customs and alleged grasp on the languages spoken inside the forest, but who clearly lacked the conversational skills required to keep danger at bay. At Ulrich's insistence Javier stepped forward, but he was a nervous type, with a twitch in his left eye and a staggering inability to inspire confidence. Indeed, on learning of his Spanish roots, Jacov had spent a frantic day attempting to find a replacement, mere hours before our initial march toward the Gualeguaychú forest, for nothing was more wretched than a Spaniard, ranted Jacov, tramping the streets of Montevideo with me in tow, nothing more abhorrent and false and laughable than a Spaniard and their relationship to melancholy, nothing more insulting and base than a Spaniard attempting to explain their relationship to melancholy because, said Jacov, it was akin to someone explaining one's relationship to a ghost or a phantom, in short, something nonexistent, since a Spaniard's understanding of melancholy was zilch. I've watched Spaniards try to invoke melancholy and it's repugnant, he said, it's a farce, he chided, a goddamn slap in the face. Turning the corner of Andes onto Río Negro, his ranting swelled, no different, I noted, than the baleful resonance of the streets, the implacable chaos, the corrugated shingling of each structure that threatened imminent collapse. I once spent a week in Madrid, he fairly spat, Madrid, do you know it? Of course I know it, I told him. All the same, said Jacov, I was on a panel discussing the abundance of anguish in Greek myth, and I saw for myself, he said, yes, I saw a typical Spaniard's ignorance of melancholy, a typical Spaniard's disregard for melancholy, a typical Spaniard's shallow and mundane reach toward melancholy, and the stench has not left my nostrils since; then, crossing Artigas, approaching the barrio of Aguada, Jacov, now fully roused, declared: in Spain I felt surrounded by barbarians, and I left the country thoroughly disgusted. The sheer abundance of self-love and aspirations toward happiness are simply revolting, he said, and it's something I've never forgotten because their incapacity to understand the details or finer points or ephemera of melancholy stands in direct opposition to our cause and my studies and my masterwork itself, he said, suddenly complaining about the rash produced by the calfskin of the *Origin Books*, which had been pressed against his stomach the entire journey over-seas as well as during our first two days in Uruguay; each time he retrieved them to jot another theory or anecdote it irritated the flesh, and I found it particularly unnerving to observe him squeezing the masterwork back into its sanctum beneath his tight-fitting vest, a vest that at one time, when Jacov was younger, would've been loose, but now pressed against his ever-growing paunch, a paunch that announced itself, in a room for example, seconds before the rest of him. Hours after hiring Javier, on our last night in Montevideo, I'd insisted he remove the *Origin Books* to sleep. You'd like that wouldn't you, he sneered, fairly accusing me of treason. Yet not three weeks later, our world had changed altogether; we studied Javier, slack-jawed and dull, as he tried to reason with the two tribes, attempting to locate the junction between three languages, all of which, it seemed evi-dent, he knew very little. An immediate feeling of disquiet emerged as the linguist tried to find any sort of lineage to human speech; meanwhile Jacov and I took turns cursing Álvaro Diego Astillero, a placid man who refused tips yet clearly demanded a much higher salary. Ultimately, we had Ulrich to thank; pushing the inept Spaniard aside, he managed to mut-ter a little pidgin and a trade was made: two pouches of gun-powder and an aluminum canteen half full of Irish whiskey for what turned out to be a great quantity of cocaine, or *coca* as they called it. It was this very trade that offended the Yaro, unknowingly of course, but it offended them all the same, for immediately after the transaction we felt their constant presence in the periphery of our travels. No evening passed when one of us—setting up the bivouac, collecting wood, tethering the asses to a tree—didn't feel the eyes of these natives watching in silence, spears at the ready, because patience, claimed Ulrich, was not only a technique they had perfected but also the zenith of their skills. Their impeccable patience, Ulrich would later insist, their unflappable patience, he later remarked, their practice of patience that isn't merely for observation or curiosity, he later said, his face ashen, his words flat and measured, but rather for the deepest understanding of their victims, for the most propitious vantage to attack their victims, which, undeniably, we are. Yes, Ulrich continued, their stealth and their silence is surely something to admire, but most of all it is their patience, and their patience is what should worry us most, for they only need to observe us for an hour, two at most, to realize we have no idea where we're going, an hour, two at most, to realize we are lost, aimless and asinine, nothing more than a clan of dolts making circles. At the time, though, the trade seemed to appease the parties involved, and Jacov, relieved to have more cocaine at his disposal, was transformed, buoyed once again into the colossus of original thinking I'd come to know and love, my miraculous master, savior of my existence, the brightest light from the highest mountain, and soon the jungle, instead of a place of *impossible* melancholy, became a place of *possible* melancholy, and I espied the spark in Jacov's cobalt eyes, the same spark I recalled from eleven years before, when I refuted the fate foisted on me by my stepfather to become a cheesemaker, telling him in no uncertain terms that I was leaving Croatia forever, that I'd found my destiny at the Holstooraf Sanatorium and Spa. Jacov was waiting impatiently outside in a carriage, accompanied by Sonja, for they had begun a passionate affair at the sanatorium, endless nights of violent lovemaking, he'd bragged, of wild contortions and animal positions that would stretch the erotic imagination to the point of fissure, since, he happily disclosed, the carnal appetites of Bohemian women were well documented, and although sex, *fucking*, as he called it, seemed the furthest thing from melancholy, it was, he insisted, one of the most refined and enlightened ways of unearthing that noble feeling, and thus, I repeated, I was leaving Croatia forever. You seem cured, my stepfather muttered, and I explained that I was, in fact, feeling better, although I felt a crisis developing in my spleen and my lower back; it was sending off sharp pains that were clear portents of an advancing ailment, one I would have to monitor closely, and it was quite possibly, God forbid, an early case of *Tatar's cough*, for a catastrophic illness is always only a breath away, I reminded him. I'd also begun to have a series of migraines, *phantom headaches* I called them, and I asked my stepfather to feel my lymph nodes, which produced an angry and guttural laugh from him. All of us, I cautioned, are dancing with death, whether we know it or not; some souls are simply more attuned to death's ginger steps, death's faint inching across the court-yard of our lives. And some souls, he groaned, perform the lead in a play nobody is watching. No matter, I told myself; outside awaited my future, Jacov and Sonja, visibly bruised by their love-making, wearing expressions of silent but ravenous yearning. One of the greater, yet less obvious portals of revealing and observing and ultimately grasping melancholy is the act of making love, Jacov said from the opposite seat, the cold breath of an early Croatian autumn finding its way inside the carriage, a cold that nestles itself into the bones, and I could feel my ancestral home getting smaller in proportion to its getting far-ther away, the same home where I'd seen my mother remarry and die soon thereafter, buried not ten steps from the father I never knew, the same village where I'd fought an array of mot-ley ailments that forced me to speculate, in reverence now, how I'd even made it to the age of twenty-four. Jacov and Sonja were huddled beneath an afghan, and Sonja, nobody's fool, said little as Jacov cursed the soil we traveled on, the trifling Croatian soil, he swore, the ponderous Croatian soil that had poisoned his existence, the exhausting Croatian soil that carried sedi-ments and dregs of the soul's damnation, and it was, in fact, only my youthful promise to be Jacov's assistant that convinced him to concede this long-winded detour to retrieve my belong-ings, for Croatia and Croatian soil brought up the most wretched and inextricable memories of Jacov's youth. I curse this revolt-ing Croatian soil, he fumed, this soil that gives me the hives, he barked, this soil that is so much weaker and more diluted and merciless than other soils. I can't wait for the moment we cross the border, because the soil of no other country is as ugly or sickly or petulant as Croatian soil; you can tell simply by looking at the ground how repellent it is, he muttered, and the moment we enter Austria, I will get off this carriage and kiss the Austrian soil, not because it's Austrian soil, which is no different than Serbian or Hungarian or Slovenian soil, but simply because it's *not* Croatian soil, and though geography, in theory, has little to do with melancholy, in practice geography has *everything* to do with melancholy, and the ever-darkening sky betrayed an optimism I felt deep in my soul, for I was leaving the home and village and stepfather who'd shown little love, only a baffling and myopic obsession with making cheese; meanwhile the carriage proceeded toward an uncertain future; the Dalmatian coast receded as Jacov berated the land of our mutual birth. I won't be able to stand myself until we cross the border, he continued, for Croatia is the source of my grief. The only thing I have to thank Croatia for is my youthful instruction in melancholy, in cultivating an intimate knowledge of melancholy. Placing a hand on Sonja's cheek, Jacov sighed the sigh of a thousand years. Lovemaking, he opined, peering at Sonja's blackened eye, sexual congress, he continued, the desire to connect with another soul, is one of life's greatest promises and thus one of life's greatest disappointments. The search for love is pure folly and making love always reveals, if nothing else, our inescapable solitude, our utter remoteness from one another. Yes, I've known melancholy from a young age, he said, switching to German, a language the three of us shared, wanting to be certain Sonja understood the origin of his life's work and, by extension, his melancholy. My dear twin, Vita, he confessed, my better half, my superior reflection, died from typhoid when she was just nine years old, nine years in which I'd known what false and comforting happiness felt like, nine years to sally the steep hills of my infernal and ponderous Knin, although not ponderous then, no, not a Knin I hated and loathed, not until it took away my Vita, my Vita and her cherubic face as she chased butterflies or birds, running after her wily and lesser twin, me, to exhaustion. Our secret dialect, our private code, our Eskimo kisses at dusk, our exclusive language that we alone understood, played out in whispers and expressions, notes slipped inside books or symbols scratched in the dirt as the locals grew more and more perturbed by our self-abdication from village life; they pondered at our otherness, wondered why we were so strange and unapproachable, why we winced at the approach of other children and found all human beings, our parents included (our parents *especially*), vulgar and frightening. The town elders wanted Vita and I to attend church every day until we became what they considered *regular,* in essence, to make us less off-putting. They wanted to divide us, to teach Vita and I separately, to have us attend different schools, thus breaking the bond of our love, for our connection waned when we were apart and, likewise, strengthened in proximity. Nothing would have made them happier than to separate us, to diminish the strength we shared, a strength they couldn't see with their eyes but that was evident in the way we held hands as we strolled through town or in the forbidden argot we invented and spoke aloud whenever a person approached. The townsfolk were everyday yokels, said Jacov, becoming more impassioned, yokels trapped in a village trapped by geography trapped in the mediocrity of its own existence. The village and its unhealthy obsession with the way Vita and I held fast to one another and fed each other not unlike the way a mama bird feeds its hatchlings, how we spoke in our own language, how we denied the existence of others; they believed it was the work of the devil. Inherently they wanted to decode or, perhaps, destroy the language she and I had invented. Her death I blame on them, on the cursed elders and my indifferent parents, who capitulated to a village full of assumptions about who we were. At every opportunity we'd escape, run to the brook behind our manor to be alone, to be our true selves, to speak our private language, for neither of us felt compelled to use the common language of Croats, and when we were asked to recite the Croatian alphabet at school we'd sneer, and often Vita would spit, and I see her now, vibrant, apple-cheeked, lifting her skirt to catch toads or cup tadpoles, to splay herself, exhausted, on the thick grass beside me or, likewise, somersault to a halt then whisper in my ear, *ughf dün stlpt*, meaning, in our private tongue, that she loved me and would always love me, and the mediocre half-wits who every Sunday worshipped a mediocre God and who stuffed the mediocre homes of Knin with their roasted rabbits and cloying stews and the odious ričet, the entire cuisine of Croatia, which I wouldn't wish on an enemy, the Croatian diet not fit for consumption, in fact a diet *at odds* with consumption, no, they would never understand because, fundamentally, their souls were incapable of understanding, but also because the language Vita and I invented was impenetrable. Her bravery, he said, her elemental soul, he confessed, her wine-red hair, he expounded, her unquestioning faith in our bond is what kept me alive. And then she was gone, he said; it took less than a week from Vita's first typhoid cough to the final prayer over her tiny coffin to make her absence from my life complete. It was no different than removing a leg or an arm, he said, or, to be closer to the truth, my heart. I was utterly bisected. Jacov scratched the thin strands of copper hair along his skull, and watching him gaze at the passing autumnal landscape, I couldn't help but find his profile the single most beautiful image in the world, a melancholic plumbing the depths of his own melancholic heart. I had death on the brain, he continued, cruel, cruel death. Sonja nodded, either enraptured or bored or traveling between the two, for she possessed a face that gave little away, and her understanding of Jacov's staunch German, with its rapid staccato and insistence on obscure words, was anyone's guess. Sonja's alluring face, her comely face, her face of confident beauty, which would beguile any man, if that was their sort of thing, a face I came to know well yet only grew more mystifying with time, akin to staring at something until the eyes fatigue and the image dissolves, for the longer I knew Sonja the less I perceived, her countenance the surface of a sea whose depths held secrets she refused to share, and thus, as Jacov confessed the origins of his life's work, she simply nodded. Phantoms visited my heart, Jacov mused, I wandered the chambers of our family manor bumping into walls. I can't count the times I concussed myself amid a solitary, late-night walk, listless, bereft, positively lost without my other half. I was an angel with one wing clipped, bumping into black walls, tapping at the doors of the sepulchral tomb that was our estate, for my family holds an ancestral name of renown in Knin; my surname is Reinhardt—do you know it? As in Reinhardt Tobacco? An enterprise whose arms extend from Eastern Europe to Belfast all the way to Stockholm, as well as to the trifling ports of Aberdeen and Reyðarfjörður; you've likely smoked cigarettes with tobacco grown on the selfsame soil that killed my Vita; thus my name, and my inheritance, has endowed me with a certain privilege: the ability to live a life of what some might consider leisure, yet, I assure you, is further from leisure than one can imagine, and as Jacov fell silent, I considered the breadth of the man who'd enchanted and dumbfounded me, for I came from a place that respected harmony and restraint and, likewise, a place that was suspicious of passion, in fact, despised passion and was apprehensive at the slightest hint of a passionate feeling for anything, music or poetry, even animal husbandry, for passion was seen as a sort of madness, an implication of lunacy, passion being the gateway to a sort of nightmare; thus Jacov's entrance into my life, with his curses against the jubilant dimwits sunning themselves at Holstooraf, was not only novel to me, but a siren's call. Alas, he continued, I had been orphaned; what once was a house made alive by my twin, my spirit guide, my superior reflection, had become a tomb; the bad spirits pounded in my ears, whispered insults ad infinitum, and my parents hardly noticed, taxed as they were by the drought that year and their obsession with the failing tobacco crops and what they believed would be the end of their prosperity. I suffered hallucinations, insomnia, and in my punitive vigil I dreamt of nymphs and cherubs floating in the limpid light, my red-haired double swimming in my imagination. In those dark times, I felt the phantom of my Vita all around me; I spoke to her in our hidden tongue, an idiom seemingly invented in the amniotic fluid, that bucolic time before getting thrust into this hopeless world, and I promised to take her wherever I went, that she would always be with me, and it was in my own wish to die that I finally had communion with my anguish; that is, I had an illumination or a premonition, a moment of clarity, and I discovered, in all its impervious glory, melancholy. When the tides receded, and I walked along the shore of my own sorrow, I discovered something sweetly profound: mankind's natural state. In defiance of good or bad news, false expectations, the ebbs and flows of regular life, if, I realized, I put all that aside, if I ignored humanity's hurried heartbeat and its hundred thousand inanities, then perhaps I could put into words this state of perpetual mourning we all felt, whether we knew it or not. Melancholy. The melancholic soul. Every single one of us is melancholic, we're inherently constructed this way, but we spend our lives busy in the act of denial, trying to deflect our most natural state, yet, if left alone long enough, melancholy surfaces; it's always there, inexhaustible, unconquerable. Philosophers have labeled melancholy a disease, claimed it is sadness without reason, yet I was certain it was the sadness *of* reason. When one is melancholic, one sees reality with complete lucidity. Melancholics are the blessed of this world, the seers and visionaries, and as Jacov spoke of his melancholy he became less melancholic, because, to study this emotion, I realized, one had to leave it behind, for melancholy drains the strength, saps the spirit, erodes the aptitude, and one of melancholy's cruelest ironies is the strength required for it to be studied. It became my salvation, Jacov confessed, and when I was old enough, I fled Croatia, first to a boarding school and later several universities, and I soon found myself in Berlin under the tutelage of the celebrated philosopher Otto Klein, the illustrious Klein, the eminent Klein, for three ponderous years before I became disgusted with Klein. Three years until I renounced Klein, said Jacov, turning my back on his flagrant anathema toward melancholy, his lack of seriousness concerning melancholy, and his self-anointment as an enemy of melancholy, three years of watching Klein take a shit on melancholy, of deferring the importance of melancholy before I took it on myself to grapple with the burdens of melancholy, melancholy and its manifold branches, an upward battle to say the least, for serious scholarship had never been given to melancholy except as a disease, and how can one expect to apply serious scholarship to a subject if the very subject you've chosen is considered the enemy? No, one must court and befriend and become intimate with the subject if one expects serious results. Otto Klein, he spat, wanted to *cure* and *abolish* melancholy, while I wished to *celebrate* and *proliferate* melancholy, and it would take years to shake the *Kleinian* influence, the *Kleinian* influence so strong it attached itself to one's every thought, to mimic and mirror and, thus, stunt any stupendous thoughts one might have, as well as the *Kleinian* scholars themselves, sheep who bowed at the throne of Klein in *Kleinian* adoration and worship, *Kleinian* followers propagating by the hour and emerging at the most irksome places, cafés and beer gardens and the glacial halls of higher unlearning, elbowing and prodding, always advancing with beer on their breath and coffee-stained teeth, chirping like idiot birds: *Have you read Klein's latest paper? Have you heard of Klein's latest escapade? Have you heard what Klein is up to now?* Charlatans, pseudoscholars, and imbeciles all, fumed Jacov, because to be a *Kleinian*, that is, a follower, a believer, a devotee of all things Klein, one had to be in opposition to truth and knowledge and a general grasp of lucid thought, and, likewise, a true *Kleinian* is morally vague, psychologically unkempt, and bankrupt in original thought, and I would even go further, said Jacov, as he went further, and say a *Kleinian* is an enemy to all serious thought. But I persevered, he said, I made my escape from Klein and *Kleinian theory*, and, despite some trifling detours, he confessed, he eventually found himself at the Holstooraf Sanatorium and Spa, collecting his wits, organizing his thoughts and fortifying himself for the approaching storm, months before he'd even begun his first serious meditations on melancholy; all he had at the time, in fact, was a collection of notes and jottings mixed pell-mell with his luggage, and I couldn't help but laugh as the natives lugged me up the hill in a stretcher, a ceiling of palms shadowing my face, laugh at the fever in my guts, laugh at my guileless youth, now fully behind me, the youth I'd entrusted, no, *bequeathed* to Jacov to use at his discretion, a decade gone, relinquished to Jacov to shape and mold like clay, to one day, perhaps, reflect his own radiant image. I'd practically reached the age Jacov was when we first met, and though my fever had likely climbed, I still had some small amount of faith, for Jacov assured us we weren't in retreat, despite the fact there was more of the original clan gone, perished from marauders and illness and abandonment, never to be seen again, than the sad lot that was left: a dozen Indians; two muleteers; that useless linguist, Javier, whose death we all quietly prayed for; and a pair of sullen Uruguayans, whose resentful eyes forced one to question their loyalty. We are not in retreat, Jacov pronounced, machete in hand, we're following the Río de la Plata, returning to the capital for medicine and supplies, his diaphanous voice reaching me on the stretcher, a pair of Indians on either side of it, carrying me, and Ulrich God-knows-where, announcing that morning he was walking ahead to survey the Río de la Plata, that futile body of water, that wretched river so wide at parts one couldn't see the other side, like an ocean, a gulf, a revolting sea, the river reflecting the horror of our passage, with the unbroken fear of the Yaro and their poisoned darts, the scattered huts that housed enemies and ghosts alike; the soul sickened at the very thought, and again he insisted we were not in retreat, we were not being hunted, although it felt as if we were, what with the Yaro's fires quivering through the trees each night, and the distressing sounds we were too terrified to contemplate. We're following the Río de la Plata, reiterated Jacov, back to Montevideo to regroup, to think things through, because I underestimated this chaotic jungle, he confessed, this demonic jungle, this heaving mass of unruly and wretched forest; this isn't a retreat, he repeated, angrier, more bombastic, more steadfast than I'd seen him in weeks, and though I wanted to have faith, I couldn't help but think we were lost, or worse, making circles, passing the same swamp, the same basin, the same clearing for days, for I was certain we had passed Libertad and

Colonia, those infinite settlements that reeked of poverty and witchcraft, and it wasn't my fever or the *phantom headaches* or my broken ankle, which Ulrich insisted wasn't broken or even twisted, but rather my instinct, a deep inner voice, that told me we were in retreat, that each time Jacov announced we *were not* in retreat, he was actually saying we *were*, indeed, in retreat, somehow apologizing for being in retreat, parading the shame of being in retreat merely by insisting we were not, in any way, in retreat, but the retreat was already doomed since I suspected a ceaseless circle had begun and we were, in fact, going nowhere, for hadn't we passed that same grove of palms yesterday? Hadn't we observed that neglected lean-to with the thatched roof just ten hours before, that cursed lean-to that symbolized all of South America, wretched and uncivilized and goading our demise? Everything resembled everything else, and turning my head I beheld Jacov, potbellied and panting, so much older than when we'd first met, though his certitude, his single-minded focus, was unchanged, stronger perhaps under the influence of the cocaine he ceaselessly snorted, refusing to admit what I already knew, that we were lost in this infernal forest, and, thinking of it now, what of Ulrich? Gone since morning, insistent on tracing the river, trekking ahead in search of approaching peril or, likewise, anything resembling civilization. I cursed his independence; I wanted him beside me to assuage my fears, to tell me I wasn't dying even though I knew I was; I'd never been more certain of imminent death in my life. In Stuttgart, Ulrich would disappear for weeks at a time, despite the fact that Jacov had bestowed him with a large swathe of land on the perimeter of the estate, as well as a cottage built to Ulrich's precise specifications, including a portion of hillocks and trails devoted to Ulrich's passion of raising attack dogs he later sold at a profit to wayward fascists and underground police. The Stuttgart property, the Stuttgart estate, where I officially became a disciple of Jacov, where I discovered the only home I'd ever known apart from my step-father's, taking that maiden voyage with Sonja toward Zagreb, where Jacov promptly ditched the carriage to spit, as promised, on Croatian soil, which, he avowed, would be the last time he would ever in his life stand on Croatian soil, a soil that destroys whatever good lies inside a person, he said, stabbing the air with his finger, and if Croatian soil doesn't destroy whatever good a person possesses, at the very least it makes the good lie dormant; it *suppresses* the good, *dampens* the good, and finally *strangles* the good to death; all this he repeated as we accompanied him onto the train, which swept us toward Vienna and eventually to Stuttgart and the Stuttgart property, so vast and colossal Sonja and I shuddered the moment we walked inside, so many rooms and halls and alabaster corridors it was like a lonesome child awaiting friends on a birthday that would never arrive, for it was only the three of us, Jacov, myself, and Sonja: me a virginal waif, Sonja still in possession of two healthy legs, and Jacov ready to clasp the kite strings of his masterwork on melancholy, our voices reverberating across the marbled floors of that modest castle, all of us unsure which room to take, for there were close to a dozen, and though Jacov and Sonja were, in a sense, young lovers, he insisted on sleeping alone, for his postcoital moods, he claimed, were erratic and often violent, and sleeping by oneself suited Sonja just fine since both contained vigorous personalities, and as much as Jacov exhibited his with words, Sonja displayed hers with silence, a silence wielded like a sword and punctuated, years later, by the thumping of her wooden leg, an apostrophe, an exclamation, a condemnation of the world's injustice; further-more, Sonja insisted this was merely a holiday, a long week-end in the country, and she had every intention of returning to Holstooraf to serve the sick and not-so-sick, the healthy and tubercular alike, as she pushed her dinner cart across the cafe-teria floor; a hiatus, she called it, not realizing the decades-plus excursion it would become. Eventually, the Stuttgart property, the Stuttgart castle, would be razed, replaced with a second Stuttgart castle that expanded in direct proportion to Jacov's ambition; neighbors died or were bought off, and Jacov promptly purchased their land; he affixed parcels and amassed tracts with no rhyme or reason, for, he insisted, he had a vision, and as long as he could attach and connect the land in the future, his vision would be attained, he'd once confessed after a furi-ous day of dictating, my vision will be fulfilled as long as the Möllers die off, for Jacov detested the Möllers, who were our closest neighbors. The damned Möllers and their wonderful land, he spat; I've been eyeing their orchard and I'd like to buy their entire plot, buy the land right from under the Möllers, who, in theory, I shouldn't begrudge or dislike, but I do, I hate the Möllers and their resplendent land, which is so much more sublime and alluring and stunning than my land, and I see the Möllers sauntering around their estate or strolling through the Schlossgarten, and I want to murder the Möllers; I espy the figures of the Möllers with my binoculars, and I seethe at the mediocrity of the Möllers, at the gift they've received and don't know what to do with; a mere whiff of the Möllers, a hint of the Möllers' shadow and I'm ruined for the day, and then he peered through the window of his study, which gazed west, directly onto the loathsome Möllers and their enchanted property. I've already spoken with their eldest son, he said; the contracts are complete, they just need to die, and eventually the Möllers *did* die and the land was bought, the orchard razed, surveyors brought in as well as Pierre Cuypers, the celebrated Dutch architect, known for the illustrious Saint Martinuskerk in Groningen, a church, declared Jacov, that transfigured the very notion of architecture, with its spires and archways and lancet windows, a building, he claimed, that conveyed the language of sadness with utter fluency, and there hadn't been a single day since he'd visited the church and found himself at the foot of Saint Martinuskerk, face-to-face with Saint Martinuskerk, that he didn't reflect on its immaculate

edges and subtle curves; Saint Martinuskerk wasn't a building
or a church, he explained, but an example of man striving for
the impeccable. Cuypers was hired and tasked with creating a
new, larger castle on the property, one that would synthesize
the melancholy of the human soul with the transcendence of
God. I want a home that evokes the unfulfilled longing of life,
he instructed Cuypers, a sullen man who groaned about the
German weather, which, Cuypers argued, was so much colder
and direr compared to the weather in the Netherlands, and
though Stuttgart had much to offer, Cuypers conceded, it left
him feeling homesick. Cuypers was charged with building the
castle in a style that, in Jacov's words, portrayed a perpetually
mocking God gazing at our insignificance; thus hallways were
built that gradually narrowed into dead ends, stairways assem-
bled to climb straight into walls; the use of borrowed light and
mute expression was prodigious, invoked in every room, giving
even the most well-balanced visitor an impending sense of ver-
tigo; every ceiling vaulted to convey emptiness and desolation,
gimmicks, claimed Cuypers, who promptly quit after six months,
asserting that Jacov was dangerous and unyielding and Cuypers
went further as he packed his return suitcase for Amsterdam,
explaining that the castle he'd been instructed to build was not
only *not* architecture but the *antithesis* of architecture and, even
perhaps, architecture's nemesis; Jacov received the news with
indifference, for he was months into his first serious meditations on melancholy and couldn't be bothered, five notebooks

filled and me at his feet taking dictation or making his coffee, rolling his cigarettes or fluffing his pillow, his imagination on fire, his mind clutching the divine, and later, less famous and less experienced architects were hired to finish the castle, and on this went for ten more years; more perverse construction, more mystifying designs that mirrored the undulations of my master's mind: the upper and lower floors as well as the cellar constructed at a subtle, nearly indiscernible tilt, and if this was due to Jacov's singular artistic vision or the inexperience of the laborers, I can't say. Already in his forties, Jacov was steadfast and indefatigable; he contained the energy of someone half his age. When he wasn't preparing his masterwork, Jacov was circling the grounds, bellowing at the masons, demanding they reach toward God but an *unsympathetic* God, he implored, a *cruel* God, he cried, a God, he howled, whose voice was muted by the *deafening roar of moronic humanity.* The castle's vertiginous contours would eventually make future guests ill at ease and nauseated, an entire estate seemingly built, said one visitor, in an epileptic seizure. Doorways led to trapdoors or false doors in maddening, never-ending riddles that took Sonja and I months to navigate. None of this, of course, took away from the sublimity of the estate itself. Unfinished, the second Stuttgart castle was still a striking and visionary work of neo-Gothic design that the locals would scrutinize in packs three, four, five times a week. Flocks of Stuttgart locals approached from the northern slope, peering at the arches and columns and stained glass of my master's home, and later came the tourists from as far away as Greece and North Africa, adorned in heavy winter coats and Verascopes. Balloonists were seen drifting past in the hopes of glimpsing the goings-on inside. And the landscape was no different: beech trees were razed, replaced by other beech trees that resembled the original beech trees but were, Jacov proclaimed, different, *more mournful* beech trees. Jacov wanted to replicate his childhood home by re-creating the brook he and Vita had once happily frolicked in; thus landscape architects were enlisted and plans set in motion to reproduce the stream where they'd shared their most intimate secrets, as well as create replicas of the hills and meadows where he and Vita first recognized their desolate place in the world and later embraced and kissed and pledged eternal loyalty. Evergreens and hawthorns and all sorts of scrub indigenous to Croatia were brought in, cultivated, and tended, exact replicas, he swore, of the cursed soil of Knin, that selfsame soil that had murdered his twin and stolen any chance he might have had of future happiness, as much a curse, he said, as a gift. All of it—the second castle, Pierre Cuypers, the landscaping, the endless masons hired and fired each week, not to mention the *meditation turret,* a stone tower affixed to the library where Jacov believed he'd receive his most sublime visions—was purchased with Reinhardt tobacco money, of which, Jacov asserted, there was no end. There is no end to Reinhardt tobacco money, he boasted, which arrives incessantly and in untold and infinite amounts I can't begin to comprehend because there's so much of it, too much to really count, which, regardless, is the banker's job and not mine, but I assure you there will be no end, no end, he repeated, to Reinhardt tobacco money, because people love their cigarettes, and as long as people continue to smoke, I'll receive Reinhardt tobacco money, and even when I'm dead people will continue to smoke, and thus the Reinhardt tobacco money is eternal and never-ending. Like stowaways, we three nested in the original castle while the Stuttgart castle, the second castle, the *real* castle, was getting built, those first years blazing with novel ideas and feelings, emotions I couldn't comprehend and to this day still wrestle with. Observing my master and his rapid production of work left me speechless. Most mornings he'd pace the Persian rugs of his study while the supple notes of Wagner purred on the gramophone, for Jacov loved Wagner, claimed Wagner ignited his imagination, asserted that he shared the same soul as Wagner or a mutual soul or a soul that mimicked Wagner's, and only Maupassant and Kierkegaard and Vita had earned that same lofty tribute, for their souls were souls at ease with melancholy, that found refuge in melancholy, that were not at war with melancholy but, instead, in *complete accord* with melancholy. And me, I once asked, does my soul resemble yours? You're a pissant, Jacov answered, flashing a sly and benevolent smile, but a lovely and loyal pissant and a pissant with promise and a pissant with unparalleled taste, and I love you, and I knew his love for me was true, for his attention to me, his dedication to instructing and elucidating the finer, subtler points of melancholy, and in the most tender fashion, had never wavered. Each day was different from the last, and on the rare occasion inspiration was slow to arrive, he would lean against the window and watch the masons at work or spy on the elderly Möllers through binoculars, for this was in the early days before the Möllers had died and Jacov had purchased their land. The Möllers are as bad as a drunk *Kleinian* he'd say, or worse than a drunk *Kleinian*, because they're not only medio-cre and insignificant, but they're comfortable with their medi-ocrity and insignificance, and I want to spit every time I see Herr Möller and his stupid mutt of a wife traipsing about the grounds of that land, that orchard that should be mine and isn't, although, of course, it eventually was. After an hour of railing against Klein or cursing the Möllers, Jacov would ease into his settee and begin muttering his thoughts on melan-choly, thoughts that at first were disjointed or muddled but would slowly become elegant and illuminating, and at this point, at the juncture between irrelevant and relevant, Jacov would tap my shoulder with his big toe, instructing me to take notes, and, sitting at his feet, I would pick up the journal and begin taking dictation. As Jacov spoke, a ringlet of light would descend above his head, and though I never mentioned it, I saw it countless times, no matter if the day was bleak and beclouded, those obstinate days of gray so copious in Stuttgart, and though there appeared no scientific reason for the halo to exist, throbbing

and trembling like a star, it was perhaps a reminder of why I fell
in love with the immensity of this great man, sitting at his feet,
speechless and astounded, while his thoughts lifted and coiled
like rings of smoke, as he raved about a new melancholy that
would one day spread across the globe, a novel melancholy that
would replace the old melancholy and all its bleak associations.
This new melancholy, he said and I wrote, would transform the
lives of every human being and slowly, as the recognition of
this melancholy grew, he said and I wrote, it would smash the
bulwarks keeping us from our superior thoughts, the melancholy that should be ours, he said and I wrote, but we haven't
yet earned, and Jacov would scratch his balding skull, and the
play of light, the smell of bitter coffee, the entire ambience was
so enthralling, for I was just a few years into adulthood, younger
than my years suggested, and observing Jacov, beautiful Jacov,
giving dictation or performing Buddhist meditations or draw-
ing up plans and notes and articles was supremely touching,
and it was impossible not to revere Jacov and worship Jacov and
wait with bated breath in deference to Jacov as I entered his
study, for Jacov was always rapturous and methodical, always
ecstatic about his masterwork because, in a sense, thinking
about melancholy, studying melancholy, *writing* about melancholy made Jacov delirious with joy. All existence is suffering,
he'd say, reciting the first of the Four Noble Truths, claiming
this was his favorite sentence in all the world, the truest sentence in all the world, the most luminous sentence in all the

world. Existence is suffering, he'd say, merely to be born is to invite suffering, to be open and exposed and unabashedly condemned to suffer; this and countless other tenets of Buddhism, he maintained, were the truest philosophies the human mind had ever uttered, composing a religion Jacov esteemed for both its simple wisdom and utter complexity. Yes, he'd repeat, all existence is suffering, and that is what makes it magnificent. Where other religions are incoherence, he'd say, Buddhism is coherence; where other religions are invested with human error, Buddhism is bereft of human error; where other religions are sated with promise, Buddhism is negation. I'm a Buddhist at heart, he once declared, peering into the Möllers' orchard with his binoculars, for Mahayana, the Great Vehicle, has taught me more than Voltaire or Klein or any of the modern philosophers, and even though I was raised in the Roman Catholic church I always felt like an outsider, for they were the most ponderous souls to walk the earth and their suffering lacked imagination; it lacked class and style. Their suffering was ridiculous, and instead of making them more sympathetic or more human, it made them look like buffoons, and even as children Vita and I loathed the churchgoers and their bad sense of theater, and during the holidays, which we dreaded as one dreads their own extinction, we would cringe at the ceremonies, the somber rituals that weren't really somber and the repugnant singing that wasn't really singing but rather a sort of tasteless sobbing projected toward an indifferent God; those songs achieved nothing but to make my skin break out in hives. The only lines truer, more peerless than Buddhist scripture, he maintained, were those penned by the unfathomable Emiliano Gomez Carrasquilla, the inscrutable prophet of melancholy who disappeared, claimed Jacov, inside the forests of South America, supposedly in a village called San Rafael, not lost, mind you, but retired, Jacov said, receding into oblivion by choice; San Rafael, a village smack dab in the middle of the Gualeguaychú forest or, more precisely, on the edge of the Gualeguaychú forest or, if we're being truly technical, *adjacent* to the Gualeguaychú forest. Carrasquilla's works on the human psyche are impeccable, said Jacov, works that tower over the paltry achievements of trivial men. Carrasquilla is quite likely a Buddhist himself, Jacov claimed, and he often gazed at the portrait he'd had commissioned of Carrasquilla, a portrait of what he believed Emiliano Gomez Carrasquilla looked like since only a single photograph existed, though by now he was decades older so any resemblance was lost, with time itself being the only witness. The portrait depicted a bald, brooding man with rustic features, a long beard, and an expression of desolation in his deep brown eyes. If it wasn't Carrasquilla or Aristotle or Voltaire or, likewise, the beating hooves of Wagner on the gramophone, it was Buddhist scripture that most inspired Jacov, who would elucidate a particular passage, often agonizing over the translation, for poor translations, he asserted, were the worst crimes an academic or a writer could commit, and a translator shouldn't be allowed to call themself a translator until their translation had been read by hundreds of scholars and for hundreds of years, so that, in short, a translator would never know if they were a successful translator in their lifetime, which, to Jacov, made perfect sense, and, following this train of thought, a translator wasn't a real translator until they died, that is, their work could only be recognized posthumously. A living translator is a contradiction, he said, and a translator, like any artist, shouldn't be celebrated during their lives since their work, their art, their translation is only being tested and, ostensibly, the test takes decades to complete, perhaps centuries, before humanity knows if it, it being the work, has the ingredients, the minerals, the muster to be called what it aspires to be called. Success and praise in one's lifetime, Jacov said, is repulsive; it's merely strutting in front of the mirror like a rooster—fun perhaps, but an utter waste of time, and anything labeled a masterpiece during the creator's life should be dismissed, just as the *translation* of this so-called masterpiece should be considered a failure if not given the time required to gestate, to be looked on and dissected and certainly not labeled a masterpiece, because the experts, and here he stressed his distaste for experts by the way he landed on the letter *P* in the word *experts*, the experts aren't really experts at all, he said, because to be an expert, like an artist or a writer or a translator, one must be read and dead for at least a century, and this meant, I thought as he spoke, that all experts and translators and artists were not experts or translators or artists *during* their lives but only after they'd died, and suddenly I knew he was talking about Otto Klein even if he didn't say the name Otto Klein, for Otto Klein was not only celebrated in all of Europe for his breakthroughs in human consciousness, but his name, in the brief period since Jacov had abandoned his apprenticeship, had become ubiquitous with psychiatry, and Jacov, by *neglecting* to say the name Klein was *highlighting* the name Klein and attempting to shame the name Klein for his enormous popularity, because for Jacov, popularity was akin to professional suicide and an immediate disqualification from serious work. Battles are waged in the academic world every day, Jacov said and I wrote; the Symbolists and the Modernists, just like me, find the *Kleinians* ridiculous and laughable and *Kleinian theory* both wretched and insufferable, Otto Klein himself being an absurd man with asinine concepts, and Klein's only supporters, Jacov insisted, were the Realists and the Stoics, who'd had a notorious falling out with the Symbolists (who preferred being called Eurofuturists), a falling out over the interpretation of a certain lecture Klein had given that argued the value of serenity in both personal psychology and larger society, all these arguments beyond the scope of my own aptitude, all these *academic tribes* utterly foreign to me, a fact I kept to myself but that hardly mattered since I was merely transcribing the words of my master and could always return to the day's notes, which I often did, analyzing and scrutinizing until my eyes hurt and my head smarted. These tribes, he said and I wrote, are all repugnant to me, and good work, authentic work, meaningful work can only be made in the solitude of one's thoughts. Among these *academic tribes*, Jacov detested Klein especially since he had once been his student and protégé. And whenever Klein's name emerged, Jacov's eyes would twitch and he would ask to be alone, and it happened that shortly after settling in the first Stuttgart castle, Jacov had the opportunity to spy on his old mentor and new nemesis, for Sonja planned to visit Prague, where her sister had recently given birth, and Jacov, chafed by the slow progress of the second castle, decided to go along, insisting it had nothing to do with Klein, who happened to be at the Fine Arts Academy in Prague that winter, where his lecture, "The Inexplicable Sadness of Søren," a meditation on Kierkegaard's moodiness, had attracted all sorts of hangers-on, explained Jacov, all types of groupies and sycophants who had converged to hear the great imposter sound off on his stupid theories, and Jesus Christ, he added, now he's brought poor Kierkegaard into it, poor Kierkegaard who happens to be dead and doesn't have a say in the matter, poor, dead Kierkegaard who can't even defend himself, but I'm not going to Prague because of Klein, he repeated, it has nothing to do with that counterfeit, that phony, that fraud. I love Prague, he said, a delightfully dismal city, a city well versed in melancholia, the mournful bridges and tragic cemeteries and woeful architecture, the sheer plenitude of melancholy and its verisimilitudes is impossible to dispute; all are nothing short of sublime. Yes, he continued, I love Prague, as well as Sonja's sister, whom I've yet to meet but I'm certain I'll adore, and newborns and travel too, I love them all, and Sonja, pale, stoic, as comely as she was silent, seemed ambivalent until Jacov displayed the Reinhardt tobacco money, which he proposed would pay for the trip, and Sonja was not only tall and exquisite, with porcelain skin and a head of chestnut hair that would break men's hearts if that was their thing, but she was a pragmatist too, and on hearing Jacov's offer, she smiled ever so lightly, dappled light the color of plum dancing on her brow and which, projected from the stained glass, gave the parlor a mood of boundless austerity, and they both excused themselves to make love, obvious by the way their eyes met and minutes later by the trembling of the walls, for their lovemaking was not only erratic and unconventional but violent too, a passion that heated as quickly as it cooled; thus Jacov could be giving dictation, espousing his concepts of mist along the Dalmatian coast for example, how this mist, when it seemingly evaporates, actually rises, attains an almost corporeal form, close to tangible, and drifts inland across all of Croatia, often settling in small villages, Knin for example, where it reappears, often heavier and more substantial, and changes the very nature of the people in the village; yes, mist, a subject that seized Jacov long before his love affair with dust, and this he could be speaking of with fierceness and fervor, and I, at his feet, taking dictation, when suddenly Jacov would twitch his nose and excuse himself, not to use the bathroom or to fuss at an architect or even to spy on the Möllers, but to traipse the entire Stuttgart property in pursuit of Sonja, to make love to Sonja, and hopefully Sonja was equally desirous, for she had no qualms about sending Jacov on his way, often with a fist to the eye if he was especially implacable, because Sonja could tangle, a skill acquired in the half-dozen Bohemian brothels she'd worked in since living on the streets as a child, a hopeless urchin, a pale slut, she'd once confessed to me in her Czech-tinged German accent that was utterly compelling if you were attracted to that sort of thing, and, likewise, Sonja wasn't lacking in sexual appetites either, for again, I could be taking dictation, perhaps counting the red hairs on Jacov's angelic legs while he spoke of the transmigration of souls in Hinduism, for example, or the melancholy of Bellerophon or the singular sadness of Mesopotamian gods, when suddenly Sonja would appear in the study, click her tongue, and I would take my leave, for I knew she wanted, perhaps needed, to make love, and this wordless compulsion had begun for them at Holstooraf; Sonja pushing the bread cart toward Jacov's table in the sanatorium cafeteria, inquiring if he would perhaps like another dinner roll, and their eyes met and minutes later both were devouring one another in his room or perhaps the broom closet or, to hear Jacov tell it, both locations as well as the attic of the TB ward, behind the topiaries, shrouded in the Holstooraf hedge maze, and various other sites both private and exposed since their passions, when heated, were relentless and often eclipsed the need or concern for privacy. Yes, Sonja explained one night, a night that found us both in the first castle kitchen stricken by insomnia, I became intimate with the needs and desires of men when I was still young, she said, much too young, but our parents were drunkards and they had jobs that they lost, and soon we were on the streets of Písek, a filthy town packed with lowlifes and illiterates, and soon after that my sister and I were abandoned. One Sabbath our parents left to forage for dinner and they never returned; we had to fend for ourselves, so we headed to Prague, which was no better, but bigger and different and it had its plenitudes, which for my sister meant a job as a seamstress and for me the giving of my flesh to men. Her attraction to Jacov, she observed, was his mania, his drive, his meticulous focus toward a goal, though, admittedly, she couldn't understand his fetish, his fixation with melancholy since she saw it as nothing more than a bad mood, a passing sadness, the ill winds of a bleak temperament, akin to the brutish tones inside a Czech tavern, so polluted and coarse and shit-stained, and I, of course, sat aghast, for these words were sacrilege; I worshipped at the altar of Jacov, who likewise worshipped at the altar of melancholy, closer to a saint or martyr for melancholy than a flesh-and-blood human, and it seemed ludicrous, even demented, that she would thrust her loins against this selfsame seraph, this mythical being, this oracle of pure knowledge but not share the same hunger for paradise; inherently I liked Sonja, though, and I absolved her of this, forever keeping her attitude toward melancholy to myself, for part of me felt her attempt to eschew melancholy was merely an escape from the dour disposition of her Jewish soul. Traditionally attractive men leave me cold, she continued, lighting one of her Dutch cigarettes; collectively I have spent weeks, perhaps months in bed with the various rowing squads of Prague, graceful men known for their fondness of brothels, handsome and lithe men so easy in their movements and fine-tuned in musculature, men at ease with their place in the world and thus nothing to prove, men whose guiding principle in life is their own pleasure and not for a second do they sense a woman's needs, *my* needs, even if they're the patron and I the product. Conversely, she added, men like Jacov have something to prove, what with his red hair and misshapen body like an overripe pear, and my body, to him, is a field of battle, a mountain to climb, an enemy nation to stake his flag into and, as Sonja continued her voice waned and, without trying very hard I imagined the rowing squads of Prague with their heaving torsos and tiny waists, perhaps as handsome or handsomer than the rowing teams from Dalmatia, whose catalogues I would order every spring as a child, more to support the organization than to look at the photographs inside, which displayed each rower's height, weight, and village of origin, the buzzed hair and downy cheeks of those virile athletes, perpetually intent and reluctant to smile, men whose well-defined loins were shaped by repetition and a hunger for victory. Men have always been attracted to me, said Sonja, but they're simple creatures; give them full bellies and an orgasm and they'll leave well enough alone, although, she added, there are always exceptions, and Sonja looked above our heads to the second floor, where dear Jacov slept and dreamt of his masterwork that within a year would fill an entire bookshelf, an entire bookshelf filled with the radical thoughts of my master, transcendent ideas on the origins and benefits of authentic melancholy, books that would one day be rendered into their most concentrated and rudimentary aspect in the *Origin Books*. But in the kitchen that night, I discerned the intelligence and kindness in Sonja's eyes, the goodwill she exuded in the silence of her thoughts, as well as her piercing intelligence, deftly displayed by her love for English poetry, Wordsworth especially, and soon we came to care for one another deeply, because my fidelity to Jacov was something she never questioned, Sonja being of a type not to query a person's nature so long as it didn't encroach on hers, and we came to an understanding that night that neither of us wanted to harm the other; in fact, we wanted to help each other, and when Sonja lost her left leg, that shapely left leg that perfectly matched her right, a luxurious leg, a ravishing leg, an alluring leg, if that was the kind of thing that appealed to you, it was as if I myself lost a leg, although that ghastly business was years away, obscured in the hazy gauze of the ill-defined future; thus, both of her legs were still attached, with blood flowing through their veins and hairs that needed shaving, legs that crossed one another that night on the floor of the first Stuttgart castle kitchen since Jacov hadn't yet acquired a single chair or table, more a mausoleum than a home, a home he promised to furnish as soon as he and Sonja returned from Prague, a trip I was encouraged to escort my master on because officially I was his pupil and factotum, responsible for organizing his ideas into notebooks, and who could know what theories might materialize on the journey? However my body was a body not long without ailment, and the *phantom headaches* I'd lately suffered had returned, as well as the cramps in my left foot that smacked of the onset of plague or consumption or even the dreaded lumbosciatica I'd long feared, and though I was guilty of fainting spells and false seizures and numbness in the thighs when there was a chill in the air, likewise in severe heat, and though I'd been warned about self-diagnosis before, the man was only a village doctor, hardly literate, a friend of my stepfather's to be completely honest, and thus I thought it prudent to stay behind and convalesce, to fortify myself for the work ahead that, when Jacov returned, as he promised, would begin in earnest, and when they departed I was left alone, save for the cheerless sound of the hammers, which occupied the second Stuttgart castle, a building that grew day by day, devouring the land on which it stood, besieged with lean and strapping men naked from the waist up, kept busy with their toils, and I wallowed in my illness as another might wallow in good health since disease is where I'd always felt most at home, and unlike

the way most viewed illness as an invasion, a close cousin to
hysteria, it felt to me like sustenance and surely the succor I
needed, and once again I found myself in the woods, Ulrich
peering into my eyes to inquire about my health, as my breathing, he observed, had slowed, and indeed I was feeling better,
having returned once more to the jungle, amazed once more by
the ceiling of trees, hearing again the songs of the toucans or
macaws or whatever damnable birds flourished in these parts.
When did you return? I asked, for night had arrived, and I
beheld our camp, where a small fire blazed and my body lay on
the carpet of earth, removed at some point from the stretcher.
Before me danced the dark silhouettes of our guides, appearing
as half-human hellions or perhaps phantoms, and I inquired
about Jacov's whereabouts as well as the matter of being lost.
Tell me we're not going in circles, I pleaded, and Ulrich confirmed that we were, indeed, going in circles, had been going in
circles, he suspected, for close to a week, and the longer we
stayed in one place, he explained, the easier it was for us to be
murdered, plucked by poisoned spears or guns the local head-
hunters used without hesitation, and Ulrich said that at night
one need only venture past the clearing less than half a league
to observe the Yaro's camps, fires blazing, which served to
remind him how far we were from home and how closely we
skirted death, fires encircled by depraved tribes, he said, mute
and unreasonable, indignant since that accursed trade, and for
the first time I longed for the provincial cesspool of Montevideo

and the evening cockfights and the paltry saloons, and then Ulrich did something he had never done before, and that was to curse Jacov, explaining that Jacov was more intractable, more unyielding, more unassailable than ever before, that the closer Jacov believed he came to finding Emiliano Gomez Carrasquilla, and thus melancholy, the deeper he dug in, more resolved to move forward, which, in this instance, merely meant a circle, and each time Jacov said we were not in retreat, that we were heading back for supplies, he was lying, and there may come a moment, Ulrich said gravely, now in a whisper, a moment looming before us like these very trees, when we'll have to go against our master's wishes, and I will need your help, and, whispering even softer now, don't say a word, for Jacov is in the bush emptying his bowels, and are you with me? he asked, and I nodded, even though it felt like sabotage or betrayal, more so coming from Ulrich, who was the most possessed and pragmatic and clearheaded soul I'd ever known, all the more onerous coming from him, since the notion of going against Jacov was more wicked than my sick soul could take, and as Ulrich explained the means of doing this, of using ropes of hemp to subjugate our master as a last resort, only as a last resort, only if every argument of common sense lost to his obstinacy, I felt even worse, because these words were spoken in the calm, life-affirming cadence Ulrich had perfected, his steady voice with its unplaceable accent that sounded German one moment, Hungarian the next, an accent that claimed three different lands of origin in a single phrase and that I'd first heard at the station platform in Tula, Russia, not far from Count Tolstoy's estate, Yasnaya Polyana, Jacov and I in retreat from Yasnaya Polyana and those cursed Tolstoyans, those wretched Tolstoyans who were after us, claimed Jacov, and who wanted us dead. Ulrich had been at the estate for months, he'd told us in that unplaceable accent, employed by Tolstoy's wife, Countess Sophia, as the most talented and admired dog catcher in all of Europe, the most imposing and formidable dog catcher in all of Europe, possessed with the means to track and ensnare wild dogs by fence or trap or poison and either releasing or dispos-ing of the dogs, depending on the client's wishes. The Tolstoy estate had run amok with packs of wild dogs, Ulrich explained on the station platform in Tula, mongrels born from the serfs' mutts and their offspring's mutts and the mutts of those off-spring, which, at that time, were going on five or six genera-tions, and these beasts were attacking peasants and landowners alike in unprovoked mobs, decades they'd been around when something suddenly snapped, as if the dogs had decided to col-lectively rise up against the hierarchy of nature. Ulrich had received a telegram in his compound at the base of Jungfrau, and upon seeing the name Tolstoy attached immediately departed for Russia. Ulrich was tasked with rounding up the serfs' bitches, as Countess Sophia called them. The root of the problem, in short, were Tolstoy's souls, his more than three hun-dred serfs, who were inordinately fond of the dogs and allowed them to procreate without restraint and with little or no structure and discipline; thus, generations of the serfs' dogs, apparently feral, ran across the countryside in packs, wreaking havoc, filching crops, attacking children, and fucking one another in the most brazen fashion. An education could be had in observing those beasts, Ulrich said in a tone of great restraint, which was the only tone Ulrich had. Dogs with no sense of order, annihilating the crops and mauling children, mocking the natural beauty of Yasnaya Polyana so Count Tolstoy could be moments from setting pen on page when a mob of these hellhounds would turn the corner just outside his window, growling, howling, barking, and shitting, perhaps fucking one another or chasing a housekeeper or snapping at the heels of one of his children, which is unimaginable but try, he urged, just try to imagine those feral beasts having sex right outside Lev Tolstoy's study as he works on one of his novels or religious works or perhaps *Ivan Ilyich*, which was remarkable, for that book was the reason Jacov had come to Yasnaya Polyana in the first place, the catalyst that had uprooted Jacov from his midlife crisis, what he called his *gray period*, the longest and cruelest interruption his work on melancholy had ever experienced, weeks spent alone in his *meditation turret*, staring, he attested, straight into the eyes of depression, and only Tolstoy and *The Death of Ivan Ilyich* had retrieved him from what he called a suicidal state, only Tolstoy and *The Death of Ivan Ilyich* had revived his soul, only Tolstoy and *The Death of Ivan Ilyich* had convinced Jacov he wasn't alone in the world, that a man other than himself had grazed and stroked and perhaps caressed the radiant light of melancholy and lived to write about it, albeit with the artifice of fiction, which, as Jacov repeatedly maintained, was the most inferior and impure of the arts, followed closely by poetry, something he enjoyed denouncing, knowing how much Sonja and I cherished verse, and often I would lie in bed in both the first and second Stuttgart castles rereading the poetry of Goethe or the love sonnets of Karl Metzler, founding member of the Dresden Three, when suddenly Jacov would materialize, insisting I read too much. You read too much, he'd say, especially poetry, those vapid, navel-gazing verses written by nonentities, but Jacov truly loathed literature, held an outrageous and lifelong grievance toward literature, most notably *The Sorrows of Young Werther*, which seemed ungodly and depraved and inexplicable since all of Europe lay spellbound by *Young Werther*, but Jacov believed the most candid and pure poetry of humankind was the poetry of psychology and science and of course the Four Noble Truths of Buddhism, of which the first of those truths was the highest, most crystalline utterance of the human mind, and on any arbitrary stroll through the first and later the second Stuttgart castle, a person might hear Jacov's Tibetan chants or the rustic recordings of Mongolian throat singers that Jacov gathered on his myriad excursions. Jacov's rancor had its exceptions though, and with literature it was *The Death of Ivan Ilyich*, and thus we found ourselves at

Yasnaya Polyana for a spell before things went awry and we fled Yasnaya Polyana, literally ran from Yasnaya Polyana to the Tula station, where Ulrich tracked us down, really no different than him tracking down the serfs' bitches. It's taken me three months, Ulrich explained, but I've rounded up most of the serfs' bitches and the bitches' pups and even the pregnant mutts and undoubtedly the sires of all these wretched hounds, this expressed on the Tula station platform, where Jacov and I were fleeing not only Tolstoy but also his roguish disciples, a crew of zealots with no sense of decency or independent thought, running for our lives from the Tolstoyans, and it felt as if Jacov and I were waiting endlessly for the train to arrive and extract us from Tula and Yasnaya Polyana and finally from Russia, because we'd been waiting for hours when Ulrich emerged and still no train, no people, deserted, simply a stationmaster with mutton-chops and a cassock coat, and it wasn't only that the trains weren't punctual, it's that they didn't seem to exist at all, as if the Tula train station had been constructed in a place where no trains arrived or departed, a time perhaps before the train was invented, an abandoned idea, a false start, though we knew this wasn't the case, for Jacov and I had *arrived* at the Tula train station weeks before in order for Jacov to have an audience with Tolstoy himself, for him to look into the prophet's eyes and see for himself the pathos of authentic melancholy. So I rounded up the serfs' mongrels, Ulrich explained in an accent that could've been Belgian as easily as Austrian or Bulgarian, because the countess, he said, was, for all intents and purposes, running the show, meaning the household, which, indeed, *was* a show with a venerable cast of religious pilgrims and hangers-on and wannabe writers and their half-dozen children, and don't forget the housekeepers and the serfs and their endless packs of ferocious mutts, who, if they happened to emerge, sent the visitors and the Tolstoys scampering, really a staggering show, and me circling the estate, killing mongrels, burying mongrels, crawling through the forest at night and checking the traps because the countess had insisted she wanted no dogs left, I want no dogs left, she vowed, not a single goddamn dog, and she was emphatic, wasting no words, telling me she didn't want to find another mongrel or she-bitch wandering Yasnaya Polyana like a rabid whore, pardon my French, she said, French being the language we spoke to one another in and that, of course, I *did* pardon her for, since she wasn't only a countess but Countess Tolstoy herself, and besides, she was the one paying me for the job, signing the check, so to speak, even though the dogs infuriate my husband, the countess told Ulrich, even though he hears the packs at night plotting in small gangs, trampling the black earth, attacking one another, his religion prohibits the killing of these dogs, and I told her I had the means to collect the mutts and move them away, since I was up to date on the most modern and scientific methods of luring and trapping these beasts, but she merely smiled, a stoic smile that expressed a lifetime of quiet diligence, then shook her head and simply said no, kill them all, insisting I wasn't to utter a word of this to Lev, not a single word about my reason for being at Yasnaya Polyana, a place of sublime peace and beauty, with placid meadows and rolling hills and verdant pastures and, of course, the magnificent birch trees, a place more peaceful than peace itself, unless, of course, the dogs were taken into account, because if the dogs were roaming, it became a place of unbridled terror, for I have tracked and caught the rabid inner-city dogs of Munich and Sarajevo and Paris, said Ulrich, and countless other capitals, but nothing prepared me for the bitches at Yasnaya Polyana, who, Ulrich claimed, were more vicious and fearless than any he'd encountered. The dogs don't belong to Tolstoy's souls any longer, they belong only to themselves; they made that clear long ago when they decamped en masse from the serfs' huts, where life was messy but good; in essence, the dogs said *screw yourselves, we'll make it on our own.* And they have. Packs of mixed breeds and half breeds, huskies and shepherds and agitated schnauzers, not to mention the infernal Dobermans, all sorts of dogs antagonizing each other, bringing out the worst in each other, for I've been doing this for two decades, Ulrich said on the station platform in Tula, a station like an excavation site, like a cavernous dream; I've followed these mongrels and witnessed the most diabolical behavior, for I rehabilitate and peddle the dogs my clients don't want, for the purposes of hunting and protection and the occasional case of companionship, but these creatures aren't fit to be taken back to my compound at the base of Jungfrau, nor my training pens in Berlin; no, they behave in a manner that insists they be put down, for I've looked into the eyes of these beasts and seen the darkness of nightmares, a darkness without reflection; I've seen the sinking of Europe in the eyes of these hounds. It was indeed Jacov's *gray period* and *The Death of Ivan Ilyich* that had brought us to Russia and Yasnaya Polyana and twice now to the Tula station; Jacov's *gray period*, where I witnessed the man I revered fall into a hopeless grotto, a sanctum with no walls and thus no way out, and Sonja and I did our best to nurse Jacov through his *gray period*, the long-winded preamble to his midlife crisis in which he was unappeasable, lost in the desperation of his own mind, refusing to leave the Stuttgart property for six months as he meandered the sinuous second Stuttgart castle, a winding abyss, a chasm of stone and marble, not to mention its slanting halls leading nowhere, replete with African masks and Hindu statues, life-size Vishnus and deities as well as priceless Persian rugs, all provided by Reinhardt tobacco money, which likewise paid the wages of the artists whose paintings and portraits, placed at inclines coinciding directly with the gradients of the walls, were gaining in number by the day, and if a morning of dictation was missed, it was likely that Jacov was modeling for a forger, for he had commissioned dozens of portraits of himself that, once complete, hung slapdash along each corridor of the second Stuttgart castle, in every sitting room and bathroom, portraits of myriad sizes and styles, some classical, others Early or High Renaissance, some insulting, others staggering in their beauty, and more than a few simply baffling in their experimentation, where a person might gaze at the portrait and believe they were looking not at my beloved master but at the explosion of a steamboat or a red barn with the doors ripped open, the thick chiaroscuros appearing to radiate, to possess otherworldly powers, and I couldn't fathom how Jacov procured all these artists, world-class forgers who emulated Caravaggio as easily as Bernini or Delacroix, all this before the *gray period*, for once the *gray period* emerged, it was a time of dissolution and grief, his discovery of *The Death of Ivan Ilyich* a true anomaly since Jacov refused to read literature, yet somehow, he'd acquired *Ivan Ilyich*, and he read *Ivan Ilyich*, and the house changed overnight, like an electrical current had been sent through all the rooms, because before he'd read *Ivan Ilyich*, Jacov was lost in the thicket of hidden melancholy. A generation older than me, Jacov's early middle age seemed to exhibit what I had to look forward to; I saw the quiet reflection that arrives when one's first chapters have already been written, when the optimism that attended younger, brighter mornings is but a vague recollection, replaced by silent grieving and crow's-feet, an aching back and legs tired from standing; no position seems comfortable, one's own body becomes ill-fitting, and the energy required to put oneself in a good mood is exhausting and worth it only half the time; all of it, simply existing, seemed like such an enormous amount of work. I observed Jacov and saw myself in fifteen years, for

Jacov, in his *gray period*, had crawled inside himself and shuttered the doors; the energy, the magnificent hysteria, was gone; he quit playing Wagner's *Parsifal*, the precursor to my taking dictation, and most mornings after I'd waited eagerly in the hall, Jacov simply sent me away with a grunt. Once or twice, at random, he'd rant about his hatred for melancholy. I can't stand the thought of melancholy, he cried, it's a punishment, a horror. I can't stand the word itself. I refute melancholy and all its trappings, for the blossoming in his soul, he confessed, had disintegrated. The blossoming in my soul has disintegrated, he said, my ideas no longer burst forth, no longer erupt but must be dragged from their graves, where they simply want to lie down and die. He stopped quoting Aristotle and began taking long walks to ponder the nature of existence, which, historically, meant the start of his musings but now resembled a desperate clawing toward a distant light. The house felt heavy from his lukewarm depression, which, he feared, was an abandonment of pure melancholy, a melancholy he believed he hadn't yet earned, and all the melancholy he'd ever felt was but practice for this pure melancholy that might or might not ever come, for I ask you, he asked me, what if it never arrives? What if the potential for pure, immaculate, and unsullied melancholy is too anxious, too unnerved to let me embrace it, and hence the harder I concentrate, the more furious my crusade, the more spooked it becomes? For that's what Jacov called it, a *crusade*, and I assured him he wouldn't fail; it was impossible because he was touched, a living saint, at least in my eyes, and there would be no faltering or fumbling but instead a period of intense labor culminating in an unparalleled work of heartrending grace, which would shake the world to its foundations and show mankind, finally, the beauty and divine nature of melancholy, and Jacov, trembling now, grasped my arm in supplication. His *gray period* had done its work; he seemed brittle, diminished, blighted by this spell or crisis, the *gray period* an ulcer that had engulfed his soul. My words, meant to assuage his fears, had done little. Inconsolable, Jacov believed a sort of deadening had occurred, something unspeakable; he feared the howling abyss, something permanent, had engulfed him. I, of course, knew better; I'd seen his soul disrobed, and without saying it, I knew what Jacov didn't: the innate pathos intrinsic to his nature, more deeply embedded than the bones themselves, couldn't be cowed nor startled, for it was more steadfast, more loyal than his own shadow. Yet some mornings I'd awaken to find Jacov on the edge of my bed, his face wet from weeping, and he appeared like an angel or a newborn suddenly aged. He stopped roaming the castle looking to make love to Sonja, for the portal of lovemaking, he claimed, had closed, and instead he sought solitude and isolation, often in his *meditation turret,* where he'd listen to Hindi devotional recordings or lose himself among the growing extensions of the second Stuttgart castle, those innumerable corridors leading God knows where, new wings constructed each year, furnished and augmented and paid for with Reinhardt tobacco money. Jacov became sentimental and would cry at the slightest provocation. On one particular stroll, we passed the replica of his childhood brook in Knin, an imitation so precise it brimmed with the same family of carp. I noticed his silence, and on facing him I saw he was crying. What is it? I asked. Those branches, he mumbled. Which ones? Over there, he said, on that beech tree; I don't know why, but they're the saddest thing I've ever seen, and he wept like a man seething from within, fumbling toward redemption but gutted by ill faith, and I gazed at the trembling branches, which I felt somehow contained the answer, or perhaps the question, as to why a chasm was opening inside my master, for indeed a hole had opened, no different than a vacuum or a void, not unlike those recent discoveries of the cosmos, a black mass where a star once existed and that apparently devoured everything in sight, even, eventually, themselves, but before they devoured themselves, they engulfed people and sidewalks and cities, entire planets, so devouring Jacov's soul was no issue at all, extremely simple business, and perhaps, I cringed at the thought, that was what had opened inside him as well. Jacov took countless walks around the Stuttgart estate, between the first castle and the never-ending scaffolds of the second Stuttgart castle, six or more years and still under construction, and amid these walks, Jacov once again remembered Vita, and sometimes during his *gray period* he murmured in their lost language, which always sent shivers down my spine, a dialect, it seemed, devised by the devil, for when he spoke in that alien tongue, his eyes gazed into a distance further than the physical world, past the horizon of the estate, pursuing the dominion where she lay. In his *gray period*, Jacov lost the thread of his life. I've lost the thread of my life, he confessed over tea, the Wagner on the gramophone turned to a barely discernible hum. I offered to rub his feet, but he ignored me, seemingly immune to my words, standing instead. The thread I've carried with me for as long as I've been alone in the world, he said, since the moment Vita caught that cough and was laid out in bed, that cough that spelled the end of her life and the beginning of my suffering, the pliant and limber thread of melancholy has been lost to me, for I'm too tired or anemic or indolent, perhaps all three, to find this thread and hold on to it. Often Jacov would contemplate the day of her funeral, and he recalled the moment she was lowered into the earth or perhaps the day before, when she was as white and brittle as a twig, gasping for air, the rattle in her chest like a coin in a cage. I wanted to whisper in Vita's ear, said Jacov, to tell her in our own tongue (a language spoken only by two; thus, her death would snuff out half its speakers) that I would never get over this, that my loyalty to her would be spent as a life in eternal sorrow, and even if this hadn't been formulated in my young brain, Jacov admitted, somehow my nine-year-old soul understood the futility of hope and the reward of melancholy. Sonja and I were paralyzed, fearing Jacov wouldn't return to his former self, that the exultant Jacov, the hysterical Jacov, the Jacov mad for melancholy, was gone for good. I still don't know how he acquired *The Death of Ivan Ilyich,* since I was responsible for purchasing books from the lists he gave me, the countless titles scribbled on streams and strips and scraps of paper, barely coherent symbols with the titles and authors of books he required, sometimes two or three times a day. The booksellers in the Schlossplatz knew me by name, for my arrival in Stuttgart was quickly followed by my finding the best doctors and specialists to look after the countless concerns of my brittle constitution, the many Stuttgart doctors and nurses I came to know intimately for all my various disorders: Dr. Krüger, for example, a lung specialist, and every Tuesday I had a standing appointment with Dr. Guesenstach, a blood specialist, and every other Friday I insisted on being bled, for I was especially concerned with my blood, feeling it was either too thick or too thin; in any case, it didn't feel right, it had never felt right, and so I called on these doctors and a handful more each week or whenever I had finished collecting Jacov's books, free from taking dictation or watching Jacov sleep, and sometimes I'd stop by simply to give my regards, perhaps ask to have my pulse taken, for disease is the perpetual state of man, and each day of good health demands an accrual. In any event, Jacov had endless credit at these bookstores, and the books were always philosophy and psychology and the sciences, never literature, so *The Death of Ivan Ilyich* was a complete mystery, appearing amid his routine stack with a deafening thump, and though it resembled all the other books, what lay inside plucked Jacov's soul, for indeed, once discovered, the change was immediate. One morning I heard Wagner's *Parsifal* trembling behind his door, and with great relief I leapt from bed and dressed, for I've always slept in the nude except for stockings because during sleep, the naked flesh mends from the day's exertions, and clothing not only hinders and slows the body's renewal but in some cases causes ill effects, something I'd argued about endlessly with my stepfather and even Jacov, who seemed dubious whenever I encouraged him to throw his sleeping gown onto the fire, but that morning I discerned Wagner and, more specifically, *Parsifal* and knew a hinge had been cracked, a floodgate opened. Jacov read *The Death of Ivan Ilyich* over and over, in his study, circling the kitchen, around the second Stuttgart castle greenhouse, and in his *meditation turret*, reciting lines and passages, and on an unusually strong binge of reading, he began copying *The Death of Ivan Ilyich* longhand in hopes, he said, that its wisdom would be transmuted to him from the character of Ivan Ilyich or Tolstoy himself, which, in a sense, was the same thing. *Ivan Ilyich* is the most perfect example of melancholy I've ever seen, he told me. *Ivan Ilyich is* melancholy, he would rave, the most undiluted, the most melodic, the most mellifluous melancholia rendered into words next to, of course, the melancholic writings of the esteemed Emiliano Gomez Carrasquilla, which doesn't really need saying, he said, but I'm saying it anyway. *Before Ivan Ilyich* there was confusion and foreboding, a Jacov cloistered by thoughts of death, by the shrill image of his dear dead Vita rearing from the abyss. *After Ivan Ilyich* there was serenity and grace, a clear vision toward his masterwork on melancholy, a sense of peace and elation, because, Jacov explained, to understand melancholy one needs to be elated, or at least content, although it helped to be hysterical, *palpably* hysterical, he added with palpable hysteria. Contentment, hysteria, and their constant oscillation are the paths that lead to the forest of melancholy, he said; without contentment, one can't find the correct path to the forest where melancholy resides, and without hysteria, one will find themselves forever lost in the thicket of ignorance, where the rest of humanity dwells. Melancholy was once again in the air, and the second Stuttgart castle buzzed. The first castle, now vacated, was weeks from demolition, and the three of us moved into the second Stuttgart castle, large swathes having been built near or adjacent or on top of the Möllers' old orchard, because, in Jacov's words, *screw their everlasting souls,* Jacov having insisted, in fact, that his study be built directly on the tract where the Möllers' orchard once stood, that orchard that beguiled and tortured Jacov until the end of his days, that orchard that got under his skin for reasons I never ascertained. Sonja took an apartment on the third floor, and intentional or not, it was the most difficult floor to divine, accessible only by a single staircase partially hidden by scalloped bookshelves and an enormous portrait of Jacov by Ludwig Boch, a stunning achievement that portrayed Jacov, looking vaguely imperial, in the vestments of an Austrian foot soldier in the trenches of battle, a sword raised high above the encroaching enemies, all of them, presumably, *Kleinians* or, at the very least, symbols or motifs or effigies of *Kleinians*, followers of that fool, that imbecile, that nonentity, and all of them enemies to melancholy; a dour, moody work save for Jacov's red hair, a red so violent it fairly leapt from the frame. This was also around the time Jacov received his first prescription for cocaine in an attempt, said Dr. Schmidt, to balance Jacov's moods and, we hoped, alleviate the curtain that had fallen across the stage of my master's mind, and Jacov's renewed exuberance for his masterwork, as well as his discovery of *Ivan Ilyich*, coincided with his use of cocaine, what he called a miracle drug. Cocaine is a miracle drug, Jacov insisted, a conduit to the gods. Cocaine has once again made me see the full breadth of my life's work; cocaine has caused melancholy to flower inside me like a field of edelweiss, but a melancholy more sumptuous and impregnable and cosmic than any I've known, and as he raved I would sit or stand, enraptured by his moods, by the emphatic belief in his own sublime ability, and I can't recall if the cocaine came before *Ivan Ilyich* or if *Ivan Ilyich* came before the cocaine, the cocaine assisting in a deeper reading into *Ivan Ilyich* or the reading of *Ivan Ilyich* somehow encouraging him to ingest more cocaine, for both had profound influences on one another, but the two were conflated, so Jacov's use of cocaine and his reading of *Ivan Ilyich* appeared as a single act conjured by destiny, and his sermons ranged from the high to the middle to the low, infinite spiels replete with menace and spleen and rancor now peppered by frequent and subsequent breaks for cocaine, so afterward he could continue with ever more expansive spiels of menace and spleen and rancor. His diatribes concerning Klein and the *Kleinians* especially, these took on an immense aspect of horror and madness, accusations and suspicions and plots of pure conjecture spewing uncontrollably and reeking of paranoia, yet with the slightest hint of truth since I hadn't met Klein but had, of course, met my master, and presumably I knew my master's soul, was intimate with my master's soul, and furthermore *trusted* my master's soul, and as such wasn't bothered much by the consumption of cocaine, because if Jacov claimed they were all brutes and bastards and *intellectual derelicts,* then by all accounts they were, and who was I to say different? Mornings I would pace the hall outside his study, keen to begin dictation and once again fill the notebooks of his ever-growing library, or perhaps finally put some order to the assemblage of shelves packed with the studies he'd dictated to me, thousands of the most beautiful thoughts and aphorisms and philosophies on that most somber of human emotions. As Wagner resounded like the boots of an approaching army, I waited in the hall with its ludicrous incline and haphazard angles, all the worse for being intentional, the new castle, the second Stuttgart castle, preposterous even in its unfinished state, and one sensed the muddle of Jacov's radiant mind reflected in the pitched interiors, in the halls that slowly narrowed, in the landings seen but forever out of reach, in the corners that caught and twisted more ankles than I cared to count, yet his mind, and my love for his mind, superseded any concerns for architecture, for what are the crude elements of the earth when placed beside the infinite? My desire for traditional dictation, however, was quickly hindered by Jacov's cocaine-addled thoughts, his desire to swim in the replicated pond or hire mediums to speak with his sister or perhaps take a moonlit stroll around the Stuttgart estate or even perhaps farther into town, toward the Schlossplatz or the beer garden or the Bruno Heinzl Tavern, where the socialist democrats, ensconced among the benches, spent their days drinking foamy beer and arguing, because Jacov enjoyed nothing more than mocking the locals, the bourgeois and the proletariat both, since he belonged to neither, insisted he was simply an artist and a psychologist and a scientist combined; thus the bourgeois and the proletariat were alien beings to him, simply herds of humans with fixed labels, not unlike the *Kleinians* or the Eurofuturists or the Marxists, the Marxists especially, who lately huddled among the coffeehouses of the Schlossplatz to argue and stomp their feet. Jacov's eyes trembled; wet from the cold, tears swam down both cheeks, for he forbade the use of a coat or even my bringing a coat, for the chill, he insisted, did him good, the same harsh chill that invigorated Jacov as he performed his Buddhist meditations in the study with the windows open and wearing not a stitch of clothing save his favorite smock; indeed, something inside Jacov had loosened, maybe good, maybe bad, and if he had been ambitious before he was more ambitious now, but it was a reckless ambition that skirted the abyss and made me frightened for our future. Having copied *The Death of Ivan Ilyich* longhand three or four times, Jacov instructed me to buy all the copies available in Stuttgart, every translation, German, Polish, and the original Russian, and while I was at it I should stop by Dr. Schmidt's to pick up another prescription of cocaine, for one shouldn't delve into one's most brilliant work only to come up short, to see the horizon, for example, to espy one's triumph, for example, to grasp the mantle, for example, only to stumble in the final stretch. At length, he concluded what I should've seen coming: he must visit Tolstoy himself, and I, of course, would accompany him, and perhaps he would pray with Tolstoy and share ideas with Tolstoy and ultimately find communion with Tolstoy, for Tolstoy was a kindred spirit who was able to communicate the vagaries of melancholy through the lesser art of fiction, and even though I detest fiction, he said, even though I loathe to read fiction, he said, even though fiction is grown adults playing make-believe and dress-up, he said, Tolstoy has captured the modern state of melancholia. *The Death of Ivan Ilyich* was placed in my hands for a reason, he stated, and as soon as he learned that Tolstoy had abandoned literature for a spiritual calling, it was like Tolstoy's estate, Yasnaya Polyana, had been waiting for him all along, for his abandonment of literature was proof, Jacov attested, of the telepathic connection the two of them shared. But at Yasnaya Polyana things had gone awry, and in fleeing from Tolstoy's followers, atop the Tula station platform, Jacov no longer considered himself a Tolstoyan but an ex-Tolstoyan or a banished Tolstoyan or, at the very least, a Tolstoyan of dubious standing, and on that platform, a train ride away from safety, Ulrich emerged, broad shouldered and hell-bent, unabashedly adroit at tracking dogs as well as people, having been sent by Count Tolstoy himself, like something out of a bad novel. Jacov unfurled a fistful of Reinhardt tobacco money in the hopes Ulrich would leave us in peace. You never saw us, Jacov suggested, winking first his right and then his left eye, stuffing the bills into Ulrich's large paw. The nonsense, the fiasco, the stupidity at Yasnaya Polyana was due to Jacov's pride; five days without securing an audience with Count Tolstoy, nothing but two seats at the breakfast table with the peasants. Our arrival was met with indifference, perhaps even disdain, which only served to exasperate Jacov, and chafed by boredom and unable to meet the master, Jacov decided to screw Masha, one of the servants, a distant niece of Tolstoy, it turned out, and what had begun as an uneventful four days, with our stay in a guest cottage on the premises, catching brief glimpses of the prophet conferring with serfs or taking solitary strolls between meals, ended with our escape on foot. At Yasnaya Polyana, Jacov was restless, plagued with insomnia and anxiety, and in futility, sheer futility, he added, I began flirting with Masha, and soon enough I had made love to Masha and Tolstoy found out, was livid, not only because Masha was his favorite servant but also because she was a distant niece, his favorite, the only one, in fact, Lev allowed to enter his study each morning to bring him his strong black tea, placed on gold-encrusted china bearing the emblem of Peter the Great, dishes which, for political reasons, Count Tolstoy felt both affection and revulsion. She always brought the count his black tea with two butter cookies and a thimble of black jelly, she confided to Jacov after they'd screwed in the guest cabin, behind the apple trees and on the shaded walking path three leagues from the closest neighbor, a patch of steppe that wordlessly evoked a sense of Russian sorrow, Jacov explained, that unmistakable sorrow so ample and operatic, an expanse of dead trees and fallow soil where nothing grew, in fact, he added, the ground seemed ripe for nothing but famine, no flowers or grass, no red clover, in short, no life, only a sort of damp marsh cloaked in Russian mist and Russian shadows and Russian despair; all the same, Masha wasn't a servant, he asserted on the Tula station platform, but a two-bit serf and a gossip. She wanted me to make love to her to inspire jealousy in the old man. Her uncle? I asked. Jacov shrugged, who knows? She was obsessed with cultural improvement and sacrifice, and what's more of a sacrifice than lusting after, perhaps even screwing, your famous uncle? I had no answer for that. Tolstoy's indignation that a stranger, a Croatian no less, had seduced and made love to his precious Masha sent him reeling, and the atmosphere at Yasnaya Polyana quickly turned sinister. From the guest cottage we observed the Tolstoyans huddled in circles, organizing in small packs, and we quickly collected our clothing and fled on foot. A carriage was obtained two or three kilometers beyond the estate, and it dropped us at the train station, where Jacov busily snorted cocaine and I anxiously paced, envisioning a crew of indignant Tolstoyans searching the village, armed with swords and pistols, a scene, it turned out, not far from the truth. To hell with them, Jacov laughed, they're pacifists, so either they come and attack me and show themselves to be hypocrites, or they confront me and turn out to be the cowards they are. His eyes were as red as his hair, and his gestures appeared erratic and magnified, his limbs seemingly moments away from turning on him. Another two snorts of cocaine and Jacov motioned me toward him with a devious smile; I believe they could also be after this, and he proceeded to unearth a golden horse from beneath his serge coat, a horse rearing on its back legs atop a pedestal. What's this? I asked. A paperweight, he said, at least I think that's what it is. Masha mentioned it being one Lev's favorite possessions, a keepsake from his campaign in the Caucasus, and when the count joined his serfs in the fields, I slipped into the study. You stole it? I asked. This needed no answer, and the golden horse, a keepsake, a paperweight, a relic more useful as a weapon than a decoration, was once again concealed inside his coat, and whether

Tolstoy wanted our heads for Jacov screwing Masha or the pillaged paperweight or both was anyone's guess. But then Ulrich arrived, at first to apprehend, then to liberate, for the moment his eyes caught sight of the cash, we knew with stunning clarity Ulrich's nature and the pragmatism with which he viewed the bundle of Reinhardt tobacco money being offered, and Jacov made it explicitly clear the bundle was but a small taste, and with little fanfare it was settled: Ulrich would receive a monthly stipend or *salary* and directly he joined us as a sort of henchman or enforcer, complicit in Jacov's myriad pursuits and jealousies and paranoias as well as the countless scores he felt needed settling, for a truce with my enemies, Jacov declared on the station platform in Tula, and they are countless and their stupidity has no depths, is simply unacceptable. Jacov considered and labeled everyone in the world, not only the *Kleinians*, as the silent and menacing mob, the formless and dangerous mob, the sly and deceitful and malicious mob, no different, he said, than the yokels from Knin, those slothful, ignorant and repellent upstarts, those world-ruiners that destroy and decay everything they touch, and not simply by touching it; no, they merely think of it and it's ruined. Suits me, Ulrich said, counting a lump of bills thick enough to clog a chimney; to be frank, I'm dead tired of the mutts at Yasnaya Polyana, the devil take them. They can keep my trunk too; I'm not going back. My loyalty follows the money, he said, and the Reinhardt tobacco money would never stop flowing, cascading in ever more generous amounts, a largesse that accorded Ulrich countless freedom for his passions, from training attack dogs to buying and selling properties across Europe, especially in the suburbs of Minsk, where he'd recently made several sound investments on a string of low-income high-rise apartment buildings, mostly housing for factory workers and broken families. I'm a slumlord, he once confessed, why lie to myself? I'm not one to paint myself as more than I am. What's more, I get bored easily. I learned at a young age that hardly a thing frightens me; in fact, nothing I know of has ever frightened me, so I look for it. Violence helps, but the boredom sets in, and I must go in search of feral dogs, who, for some obscure reason, soothe my nerves. Yet in the Gualeguaychú forest, with only a tenuous grasp on reality, I now saw Ulrich faced with the one thing that frightened him, and that was betrayal, for he kneeled beside me and insisted I choose sides, that I help him when the moment came, and I felt clammy and cold, and though I urged him with my eyes Ulrich was resolute; even though I felt my lungs filling with fluid, a sure sign my TB was finally arriving, that and the tingling in my toes that was either botulism or the dreaded *Tatar's cough*, Ulrich wouldn't hear a word of it. We could be attacked at any moment, he said; tomorrow I will nudge our route just the slightest, taking us, God willing, out of the Gualeguaychú forest and returning us once more to San Rafael, and I remembered the shanties and huts of San Rafael and our troubles with the locals when we first approached through the fog, all of us mud-stained and delirious, resembling a sort of apparition, for in truth, I couldn't say how long we'd been out in the elements because we'd existed in ceaseless perdition, damp earth attached to every facet of our existence, from our boots to our clothes to our faces, making us all resemble one another, and who could say how the hours divided themselves into days or weeks or months? We'd left Montevideo almost five months before, and I was almost certain we'd left Uruguay, perhaps breached Argentina or gone north by mistake and entered Brazil. Who knew? All of it a blur of wilderness and fog, weeks of fruitless searching for San Rafael and Carrasquilla, then fruitless searching for Carrasquilla and San Rafael, all under threat of death, with the veiled arrows of the Yaro pointed at us. San Rafael was the village we'd searched for in vain until, by pure dumb chance, we'd found it, the village where Emiliano Gomez Carrasquilla, the great shaman of melancholy, supposedly resided, and when Javier, that hack interpreter, as Jacov called him, spoke his first words to the locals, chiefly Emiliano Gomez Carrasquilla's name, we thought we'd met our end, for a trio of ebony-haired locals unsheathed pistols from beneath their ponchos. You're the most abhorrent interpreter on earth, Jacov told Javier, the most hateful and dangerous interpreter, he spat, an interpreter who invites our deaths with every word you speak, as if you want, instead of bringing us closer to life, to bring us closer to death. Before finding San Rafael we had almost given up; Jacov was chewing four to five balls of coca a day with much less effect than his Stuttgart stash; this and the plenitude of rain forest, with its verdant green and wavering light, had become his personal tormentors. The endless mist that hovered in the air and covered life's every detail Jacov took as a personal affront. His withdrawal from the powerful Stuttgart cocaine sent him reeling, and he raved about the repugnance of South America, a land, he said, a continent, he insisted, that shows its depravity by hiding its best minds, most notably Emiliano Gomez Carrasquilla, the greatest, most astute observer of melancholy of the past century. Then we stumbled upon San Rafael, evident from the wooden sign that read San Rafael, but the fortune at having found the great philosopher's village quickly soured when Javier attempted to communicate, causing an already irate Jacov, a Jacov trembling from cocaine withdrawal, to curse the incompetence and ill fortune of hiring Javier in the first place, for the Spaniard was so inept our energies were spent as much on keeping him silent as his were spent misspeaking the obscure dialects spoken inside the forest. At every opportunity Jacov would berate both Spain and the language it produced, a stupid language, he spat, even the natives in the woods know enough not to speak. To hell with Spain, Jacov seethed, to hell with the nation that birthed you and Madrid, that armpit of a town, that scab of a city, that unmitigated wound on Europe and the earth! Madrid is what happens when millions of idiots procreate and their children, even worse idiots, also procreate, fucking being perhaps the one thing you Spaniards are any good at, and when I was in Madrid my soul ached and time simply stopped, as if I'd been sent to hell, for Madrid is the archetype of hell, Madrid is hell's simulacrum, for they share every detail, every imaginable facet, and if I had a choice I wouldn't even murder you but simply send you back to that accursed land, which, in the end, is what you deserve, and you're so stupid you'd probably enjoy it, this final jibe was promptly followed by Jacov cramming a ball of coca in his mouth. Initially, the signpost reading San Rafael had been spotted and Jacov felt everything was saved. Everything has been saved, he roared to the dozen of us that remained, his voice permeating the fog like a specter, for lately our days had been spent at high altitudes, the mist so thick at these elevations we caught only scattered glimpses of one another, each day concluding with the realization that another person had vanished, deserted perhaps but more than likely fallen off of a cliff, the mule having no notion of where earth stopped and death began. San Rafael was most certainly the place, Jacov felt, where we would find Emiliano Gomez Carrasquilla, the lost prophet of melancholic philosophy whom Jacov had first discovered when he'd left Knin at fourteen to study at the elite and noble Harmsgradt Institute and Gymnasium outside Bucharest, a private college of which past luminaries included violinist Rolf Brâncoveanu, communist leader Mircea Bogdan, and theater critic Andreea Antonescu. At fourteen Jacov was an outcast, a self-appointed pariah, willfully renouncing the Croatian alphabet, speaking instead the language he shared with Vita, not merely dotting his speech with phrases but rather speaking *solely* in their tongue; in short, ignoring Croatian altogether, speaking emphatically and articulately so that the more he said and the more passionately he said it, the more convinced the villagers became that Jacov was possessed by the devil, and his parents wished nothing more than to send him away, for it had been more than four years since Vita had died, and instead of convalescing and maturing, Jacov had grown more isolated and anguished, as if the death of his twin was an injury newly born, and it was a stifling night in June when he approached his parents, who sat before the great barren fireplace, and explained in the most clear and precise Croatian they had ever heard, a pronunciation like that of a great orator or an actor reciting Goethe, not to mention a language they'd not heard Jacov speak in over three years, that he would indeed leave Knin, as both they and the village, in fact, as all parties involved, wanted, but he insisted he be sent to the Harmsgradt Institute and Gymnasium, of which his parents knew not an iota, had never even heard the name spoken, but they happily agreed, relieved their son was absconding from the village, although not a little horrified by the duplicity of his nature, which appeared as quickly as a change of clothes, what his father once described, Jacov bragged, as *a snake shedding its skin.* At fourteen Jacov left Knin; by fifteen he'd already read the first work of Emiliano Gomez Carrasquilla, the pamphlet *How Joy Saves Us*, left inadvertently on a table in the Harmsgradt library, a work that didn't mention sadness or pathos or, indeed, melancholy, but a short philosophic work that, like its title suggested, was a guide to experiencing joy as well as the importance of bliss in one's life. All of Carrasquilla's works, in fact, from his treatises to his aphorisms to his larger, late-period masterworks, were testaments to the glory and profundity and sheer significance of happiness. This struck young Jacov, a depressed and semi-suicidal Jacov dressed all in black, a Jacov who mumbled in a solitary tongue while eschewing his classmates, preferring instead remote swathes of campus where he could ruminate in the shadows, as the work of a visionary and living genius, and instantly he sensed the life-changing effects Carrasquilla's works would have, for he said, and I wrote, I sensed the irony in Carrasquilla's tone, this and more dictated one morning in the second Stuttgart castle as I gazed upon the crown of Jacov's head as if it were a radiant planet I longed to inhabit, not only an irony, he continued, but a subtlety, a nuance, an acuity all the dreary and bleak European intellectuals lacked, for what they said and wrote, he said and I wrote, I had long understood, and their redundancy was made more palpable by Carrasquilla's exquisite works, which showed the aesthetics of an original mind, for Carrasquilla was a reformed theologian, a mystic, and this mysticism informed all his works, imbued his meditations on happiness with undeviating originality. Carrasquilla had gone through all the trials, from Stoicism to

Shinto to Hinduism, until finding contentment in the simple act of isolation, and a divine path, melancholy, had presented itself. In the Romanian countryside, Jacov said, my soul burst forth; in the Romanian countryside, he explained, instead of simply feeling melancholy, I *understood* melancholy; in the Romanian countryside, he continued, my dear dead Vita found a cipher, and through the words of Emiliano Gomez Carrasquilla, all of which I associate with the luminous Romanian countryside, where, if one speculates on the existence of the divine, one need only spend a night in the Prahova Valley, where the light marries the cliffs to the soul, to feel the solace and harmony of the divine spirit, I found comfort. In that valley I experienced a moment of self-transcendence and understood my life's purpose. I could finally speak about melancholy on an intellectual level because in the Romanian countryside, Carrasquilla had bestowed on me the necessary vocabulary, and each time Carrasquilla used the words *joy* or *happiness* or *contentment*, I simply inverted them. Everything Carrasquilla wrote, Jacov explained, celebrated life and the joys of existence, from the daily ritual of a warm meal to the beauty of contemplation, and in my deepest soul I knew he was ridiculing and mocking those who pursue happiness, and so, in short, his attention to happiness and his eschewing of melancholy was merely a clever way to eschew happiness and attend to melancholy. Thus I searched for all of his works and devoured all of his works, and while I did this I merely transposed, that is, I inverted, everything he wrote, which, I'm certain, was Carrasquilla's point, for as well as being the greatest melancholic philosopher in history he is also an astute humorist, and so his words of joy were actually words of pathos and lamentation, and I realized, at age fifteen, that I was the only person to understand this; not even his German translator, Elsa Weber, understood or appreciated the fact that in her adherence and fidelity to his work, she was literally translating the *inverse*, the *opposite*, the *negation* of her author's intentions! In the architecture of Carrasquilla's work, said Jacov, I understood his *negation* of melancholy was actually an *endorsement* of melancholy; his passion for joy was actually a suspicion and a distrust and a weariness of joy. Everything he wrote, when reversed, formed the most radical and shrewd philosophies I'd ever encountered. His largest work, *Why We Live*, once inverted by me to *How We Die*, is the best example, a six-hundred-page theory on the purpose of finding happiness, meaning a six-hundred-page theory on the purpose of losing happiness, or rather, finding melancholy, and as Jacov spoke tears streamed down his face, for whenever Emiliano Gomez Carrasquilla's name was articulated, it was hardly possible for Jacov to contain his emotions, so beguiled and spellbound was he by his mentor, and sometimes he excused himself to make love to Sonja, for the melancholy that attends postcopulation is one of the greatest and most serene melancholies to exist and should always be strived for, and this, he said and I wrote, can be found in many of Carrasquilla's pamphlets on self-restraint

and his conviction in the joys of celibacy and abstinence, meaning his conviction in the anguish and grief of sex. Each time
Carrasquilla mentioned abstinence, Jacov said, I replaced it
with sex; each time Carrasquilla mentioned joy, Jacov revealed,
I replaced it with melancholy, and when Carrasquilla preached
moderation, I exercised the most radical debauchery; so you see,
he said and I wrote, his works were the catalyst to my visiting
and later pillaging the bathhouses and bordellos of Bucharest,
where the women were as cheap as they were beautiful, silky-
skinned mammals who taught me the immutable sadness that
permeates the soul immediately after climax. From them, Jacov
opined, I discovered the violence inherent in intercourse, and
my predilection for slapping and spanking and punching soon
followed, for Carrasquilla is also an emphatic pacifist, meaning
a warmonger. My sixth autumn in Stuttgart had arrived when
Jacov dictated to me his discovery of Carrasquilla: the long sad
years at the Harmsgradt Institute and Gymnasium, where
alone he tramped the Prahova Valley, a valley imbued with the
most concentrated beauty on earth, an ambience of pure bliss,
which inevitably produced unmitigated sadness, Jacov's only
solace being the works of Emiliano Gomez Carrasquilla, and
ultimately he left the institute without a degree, tramping
about greater Europe and fornicating his way from Vienna to
Stockholm to Belfast, acting out, he said, the opposite of everything Carrasquilla wrote, and with each new work, with each
new translation, he felt closer to Carrasquilla or, rather, to

melancholy, which amounted to the same thing. He considered *The Abstinence Sequence*, a series of pamphlets published in 1893 and renamed by Jacov as *The Fornication Sequence*, especially blissful, and yes, he said, I fell in and out of love, and yes, he said, there were dozens, perhaps hundreds, of women I became melancholic with, but the only constant, he said, my unflinching northern star, was Carrasquilla, whose works I would read and invert whenever I was holed up in a cheap flat or some dismal boarding house, for I was destitute and hadn't yet inherited the tobacco money I would later find so useful, my mother still being alive, my father having died shortly after my escape from Knin; my mother would send small checks with tiny notes and pressed flowers because the poor woman had become sentimental and sappy in her old age and looked back fondly on a time when we were as mother and son should be, meaning a time that never existed, and thus, being impoverished, I traipsed about the greater and lesser cities of the continent. I copulated with fat women, skinny women, old women, widows, and spinsters alike, fornicated with wealthy and complacent women, all to unearth the melancholy at the root of joy, or perhaps the joy at the root of melancholy, because the order, he said, has always been immaterial. The more Carrasquilla's writings provided a path to euphoria, Jacov said, the more I fornicated to find pathos; the more illuminating his philosophies on bliss, the more determined I was to screw myself into sadness. The breadth of all those milky arses and breasts, Jacov reflected, all those supple limbs, all that copulation from Leipzig to Bristol to the shores of the Black Sea, martyring myself at the throne of melancholy, where soon enough I became a man. I joined the Symbolists for a spell, then the Stoics, a detestable clan, who were worse than the Realists, who loathed the *Kleinians*, whom I joined and later renounced, a rather scandalous business that caused no small amount of gossip in the better universities along the Danube. But I was evolving. I discovered opera, mainly Wagner, and if the sound of melancholy was Wagner, the color of melancholy was Caravaggio, the most brutal and visceral painter I've ever known, whose visionary works swam before my eyes like divine light: those fleshy archangels, those pious wounds, the play between dark and light, and suddenly I understood Jacov's motivation for all those imitation Caravaggios punctuating the walls of the second Stuttgart castle, most featuring Jacov in celestial light, visited by angels, and one in particular, clearly a rip-off of *Mary Magdalene in Ecstasy,* exhibiting, in her stead, Jacov in ecstasy, his graceful brow steeped in the deepest chiaroscuro and winged cherubs circling his ankles, and I appreciated how the reproductions of his idol had found purchase along the walls of his home, for anything that brought Jacov closer to the experience of reading Carrasquilla or hearing Wagner or observing Caravaggio, in a word, closer to melancholy, my master would assail without restraint. All the same, he continued, I became refined. I knew if a brothel was worthy of my attentions simply by the slant of its awning or the font of its signage. I understood the ceaseless cadence of a city, for just as Emiliano Gomez Carrasquilla was an ascetic who practiced self-denial in the backwaters of South America, I inverted this, and thus I lived in the bustling centers of Europe as a shame-less profligate, not for joy, he said, not for pleasure, he insisted, but for the highest, most lofty emotion any earthly and terrestrial being can achieve: the ever-giving transcendence of melancholy, and Jacov wept and I grasped his thigh, never wanting to let go. Twice a year a new translation of Carrasquilla would suddenly turn up, and twice a year Jacov found himself cloistered in a cheap Munich flat or some prostitute's den in Graz, reading and deciphering the words of his model and mentor and melancholic seer, and the feelings Jacov had for Emiliano Gomez Carrasquilla were the selfsame feelings I had for Jacov, for Jacov expressed these emotions clearly and acutely and yet, when I tried to express this semblance, Jacov placed a pudgy digit on my lips as if to say, *I know, my child, how could you not love and revere me? Now is not the time.* Outside, destruction of the first Stuttgart castle was almost complete, and above the clamor of demolition Jacov told me to take note, and he began to illustrate the early 1890s, a time when hedonism was con-summated and celebrated without restraint, and though I was merely a boy in the early 1890s, I felt a nostalgia for the early 1890s because, said Jacov, the early 1890s was a time of the greatest debauchery and excess, meaning, to him, a time of delving into the tumultuous and depthless waters of melancholy;

the early 1890s, he said, a time of endless copulation, almost always with strangers, to find a portal to melancholy, melancholy found in the sultry bathhouses of Romania and Germany and Austria-Hungary and melancholy found in the masturbatory works of Carrasquilla, whose best and brightest and most acute insights into happiness, thus melancholy, were symbolic of the early 1890s, but especially 1894, because, Jacov pointed out, 1894 was like an orgy of boundless sex, unconstrained melancholy, and little else. The year 1894, Jacov illustrated, was three hundred and sixty-five days of unfettered and lawless and incomprehensible sex, and, he added, unparalleled melancholy if you knew where to look. It was a time, Jacov said, when I was collecting the foundations for my later work, for I had only recently met Otto Klein and been introduced to *Kleinian theory* to later refute *Kleinian theory, Kleinian theory* helping my growth as much as hampering my growth, but at the time I was maturing, I was filling out, and my bones were setting themselves and my focus was sharper than ever, and suddenly Jacov stopped because Sonja appeared in the doorway, for she hadn't yet lost her leg and could approach unannounced with great stealth. She and I had been trading books of English poets, which infuriated my master but delighted Sonja, who at the moment was returning a book of Tennyson I had lent her, always with the addition of marginalia, for Sonja was not only an incisive reader and translator of verse but also a talented poet herself, and later, after the loss of her leg, when her poems took a rather foreseeable turn toward darkness, there was great beauty in her work, for Sonja saw the surface of life but also perceived the inner workings of the soul, and unbeknownst to Jacov, her Czech translations of Coleridge's *Lyrical Ballads* as well as *Kubla Khan* had found small publishers, were recognized and highly sought after, although available only in obscure and provincial bookshops. Her earlier poems, surprisingly, contained a pastoral element, a love of meadows and hills and a lyrical fondness for animal husbandry, surprising for Sonja, an urban creature, a girl of the city, and even in her time as both lover and housekeeper for Jacov, she didn't refrain from her cultivated comforts but instead frequented the bistros and cafés of Stuttgart, where she befriended artists and revolutionaries and subversives alike, for Sonja adored the Decadents and was especially enamored by the works of Swinburne and Verlaine but found melancholy dull, a dead end, whereas myself and Jacov found melancholy endlessly alluring, a gateway to the human spirit and quite possibly the most beautiful and poetic word to ever pass from human lips, for the study of melancholy, Jacov once stated, was an act of intellectual grace, and merely uttering the word slowly, *mel-an-choly*, invoked a palpable vision of an apple-cheeked Vita running across the tawny fields of Knin, which was no different, claimed Jacov, than seeing the face of God. The year 1894 was a squall of debauchery, Sonja cursed, having obviously overheard us, and your *search* for sadness, your *journey* into melancholy, left cities like Prague, and women like me, maimed and syphilitic. Jacov swatted away her words. Sonja sipped her schnapps and handed me back my Tennyson. Even I, she said in parting, being a sexual creature, know my limits, and 1894 is a black mark on the history of the earth. She exhaled a lungful of smoke and retired to her apartment, where a young man likely waited since her relations with Jacov had always been open, and what's more, Jacov had lately grown indifferent to sex, the source of this indifference being a mystery Sonja had no ambition to solve. Sonja enjoyed nothing more than entertaining young Stuttgarters, to awaken their most carnal desires, and I often saw these lovers afterward, lost in the intricate wings of the second Stuttgart castle and looking for an exit, and I did my best to guide them out, young virile men sheathed in sweat, pupils engorged, and I didn't know what they did with Sonja but I could've imagined, just as I imagined Jacov in the various positions a man of such beauty held in repose or perhaps in copulation or, if I imagined harder, climbing a tree, for why not, why couldn't Jacov don a pair of breeches and take an excursion, allowing the sun to envelop his doughy thighs and pale shins as he grasped the lowest branches of, say, a pine or a beech or a spruce sapling, lifting himself, grunting, off the ground? These young men, bruised and blemished, fled the second Stuttgart castle, and I never saw the same one twice, and to be perfectly frank they weren't always so young, as I had seen Sonja ushering seedy men and dissolute men and drunkards alike, men who proved her tastes weren't always so meticulous, and whether she enjoyed the slapping and punching so cherished by Jacov is a mystery, but her taste in men, like Jacov's in women, ran the gamut and I often wondered if Sonja brought the same passion and invention she had for verse to the bed, but I dwelled on this only a moment, for the sun had risen and Jacov stood above me; the hair around his ears appeared as flames, and he placed his palm on my forehead, insisting my fever was gone. Your fever is gone, he declared, we're leaving. Turning my head, I saw the hooves of donkeys and the feet of our guides, and once more I was returned to the cursed soil of South America, the cruel soil of the Gualeguaychú forest, the same soil I prayed would envelope me, for how many times can a man court death, how many times must a single soul suffer the indignities and fevers of existence? Jacov held a machete in his left hand and the *Origin Books* in his right, for it appeared he had just finished taking notes or perhaps sketching landscapes, as had been his habit of late. We are not in retreat, he muttered either to me or the fog or perhaps to himself; no, he insisted, we will find our way back to Montevideo to gather more supplies, cocaine especially, and I wondered if Montevideo was days or months away, because the landscape of this continent was infernal and endless, had coalesced into a single drawn-out moment and, if pressed, I would've sworn we were repeating ourselves, rehashing events, ascending the same hills, passing the same lean-to, condemned to cross this cursed land in perpetuity. I sat up. Jacov receded and a moment later Ulrich was beside me; it's time you walk on your own, he said, we can't be hampered by your illness any longer. I will nudge us toward San Rafael, he whispered, where, God willing, we can placate the locals and send word where we are. A mule defecated beside me. An ancient bird cawed overhead. The fog was a solid object, fixed and intractable, and I didn't recognize the surroundings as earth but as the outlandish terrain of a land attempting to repel us, and suddenly a Uruguayan guide was beside Ulrich, insisting neither San Rafael nor the Río de la Plata was anywhere in the vicinity, and why, he asked Ulrich, why are you so obsessed by these places? This set off an argument between Ulrich and the Uruguayan guide about the river beside us, which Ulrich insisted was the Río de la Plata and which the Uruguayan guide assured him was not in any way the Río de la Plata, as we hadn't been near the Río de la Plata in months, literally months, and the Uruguayan guide laughed in Ulrich's impassive face at the sheer amount of time and distance that separated us from the Río de la Plata, and you seem to be a reasonable man, said the guide to Ulrich, you seem to be an educated man, said the guide to Ulrich, yet you somehow believe we've been beside the Río de la Plata, *hugging* the Río de la Plata, *touching* the Río de la Plata all along. All of this, of course, badly translated by Javier, who couldn't help but laugh at the Uruguayan guide's brazenness, all of which strained Ulrich's already fixed jaw. We separated from the Río de la Plata almost sixty days ago, the guide told Ulrich and

Javier translated, sixty days during which the brush has grown thicker and the hills steeper, he said and Javier translated, sure signs we're in the deepest innards of the Gualeguaychú forest, those were the exact words Javier translated, *deepest innards*, sixty days in which, if you'd been paying attention, you should have learned the estuary we're now parallel to is in no way comparable to the Río de la Plata, the guide said and Javier translated; in fact, I plainly remember explaining the difference between this river and the Río de la Plata, the Uruguayan guide concluded and Javier translated, illustrating the most extreme, most profound contrast of both flora and fauna between both rivers, among numerous other details, and like a vision Jacov appeared, insisting none of that mattered. None of it matters, he said to all present, which, due to the fog, was a mystery, as there could have been ten or twelve of us remaining as easily as four or five, because the impregnable fog meant faces could appear or disappear, arrive and depart, come and go at will, and spontaneously too, making the entire spectacle resemble the rehearsal of some second-rate tragedy. It's all irrelevant, said Jacov, the rivers and their names, the obnoxious climate, even the direction; no, what matters is finding Emiliano Gomez Carrasquilla and thus unvarnished, impeccable, and unassailable melancholy, and only the congruence of these things will bring us closer to our destiny, and if Carrasquilla has returned to San Rafael, we will return to San Rafael and retrieve him but not before we visit Montevideo for more cocaine, and I shuddered with revulsion, for I remembered San Rafael and the witch doctor with filed teeth who breathed smoke in Jacov's mouth to decipher his soul. Upon our arrival, we were told Emiliano Gomez Carrasquilla had been run out of the village only weeks before, and Jacov, having just missed his mentor, was beside himself. He fell to his knees and wept; he wrestled with himself and kicked at the sky, and whatever threat the villagers believed we posed vanished immediately, except, of course, the threat posed by Jacov, whose theatrics piqued the interest of the witch doctor or medicine man or village elder, who insisted he read Jacov's soul, for he was certain it was the soul of a sick man, assuring us the ritual wasn't an exorcism but an examination of a person's vigor and intentions, at least that's what Javier translated, although in the past, Javier admitted, he'd often confused words like *exorcism* with *river* or *monkey*, strangely intricate and complex words, he explained in German but with a Spanish accent so dense it was impervious to scrutiny. By breathing smoke into the nose and mouth of his subject, the witch doctor or medicine man or village elder would observe the corpus, the good or evil contained within, at least that's what Javier translated, although there were certain words, Javier confessed, thorny and delicate, which posed problems, words like *food* and *sun* and especially *God*, for, Javier noted with surprise, they have so many words for God! None of this mattered to Jacov, who was eager for the ceremony, happy to ingest anything that had the slightest

chance of rivaling his beloved cocaine, the drug that chan-
neled, he asserted, the most audacious strain of melancholy
ever known to man. It was the same ritual they had performed
on Emiliano Gomez Carrasquilla weeks earlier before expelling
him from the village, for the witch doctor or medicine man or
village elder had sensed the most concentrated evil inside
Carrasquilla, translated Javier. We forced Carrasquilla to leave,
explained a dark-skinned woman with painted limbs, even
though he'd lived among us for years and was a man at the end
of old age, she said and Javier translated; we don't tolerate the
presence of evil in San Rafael, she said and Javier translated,
for the old man had begun to exhibit signs of violence and
aggression and was no longer the tranquil man who once
joined our village, the same man, she said and Javier translated, who once taught the children, including me, how to read,
and Javier appeared drained from all the translation, doubtless
the most he'd done on our journey, and I remember gazing at
the adobe huts and the hungry goats and finally at the witch
doctor or medicine man or village elder, whose filed teeth were
like the teeth of a shark or a bat. Now, of all places, Ulrich
wanted to return to San Rafael, for he swore he'd spied the
presence of a telegraph. I spied a telegraph, he said, but whether
or not it works we'll have to see. And what kind of welcome
could we expect to receive? I pondered, staring at Jacov, whom
the witch doctor or medicine man or village elder had decreed
was as ripe with wickedness as Emiliano Gomez Carrasquilla

had been, the first man to speak to my master's soul, now roaming aimlessly in the jungle, likely crippled and infirm, perhaps on his last legs. Emiliano Gomez Carrasquilla, the same man who inspired Jacov to travel across Europe in search of melancholy by fornicating and deciphering his works on joy and exhilaration. After six years of tramping and reading or reading and tramping, he said and I wrote, the books stopped coming. Yes, Jacov explained one evening as he warmed his feet beside a fire in the second Stuttgart castle study, the books suddenly stopped, stopped arriving or getting published or, at the very least, getting translated, and I let a year pass and then two years pass, but after three I panicked, for I feared Carrasquilla was dead. And I asked myself, said Jacov: Had he died? Immediately I answered no, Carrasquilla hadn't died, for I would've felt it, would've sensed the earth shift, would've felt the legions of black birds take flight as they did when my dear Vita died, and Jacov uttered a prayer in their lost tongue, fierce, guttural sounds resembling the braying of sheep, much like the sounds of my youth and my insipid stepfather, the cheesemaker, and his absurd fixation with the perfect Pag cheese, how he'd awaken in the middle of the night to milk the sheep to make the purest and most impeccable cheese, countless sheep ludicrously pervading my youth, and all for the sake of making cheese, the perfect Pag cheese of my lousy youth, which sent shudders across my entire frame when, as an adult, I passed a cheese shop, any cheese shop, and saw reflected back my own sorrowful childhood. I was on the cusp of thirty, said Jacov, and I looked back on the second decade of my life as a chapter I was only too happy to leave, for I had been marked permanently by the early 1890s and especially 1894, for those years, the early 1890s and especially 1894, were the dues I had to pay to understand the responsibilities and obligations and burdens of melancholy. Having spent her widowhood like the rest of her life, that is, in Knin, my mother finally expired, Jacov said and I wrote, and having acquired, that is, inherited, all the Reinhardt tobacco money, I settled for a while in Zürich, but fearing the boundless temptations of that town I left for Belgrade, where I bought a house and hired a housekeeper. I built a study where the focus, for once, was not melancholy, which I begrudgingly put on hold, but rather on discovering everything I could about Emiliano Gomez Carrasquilla, for I had to know the source of this man and why his books had stopped getting published, or worse, why he stopped writing them. Emiliano Gomez Carrasquilla was, Jacov said and I wrote, a mystery, but more than that, his works themselves were mysteries; how had they managed to be translated, and moreover, how had they found their way to me in the far-flung halls of the Harmsgradt Institute and Gymnasium? Carrasquilla, a phantom, a mystic and visionary, and my beloved spirit guide, all contained in a single person. A man whose works were surely enough by themselves; however, with no new books, I was desperate to find out for myself the character and the substance of Carrasquilla, for what had become of him and his obscure legacy? Amid the countless burdens the world hands us, he said and I wrote, through all the impediments, seen and unseen, good and tragic, feeble and stalwart and unabashedly cruel, he said and I wrote, somehow this man had been translated and published, and somehow his books had found their way into my young heart. This dictated to me only days after Jacov and Sonja's return from Prague, where Sonja had met her newborn niece and Jacov had spied then approached then attacked Otto Klein following his lecture "The Inexplicable Sadness of Søren," which Klein survived with only the slightest injuries except, Jacov maintained, his wounded pride, for Otto Klein couldn't help but discern, Jacov said and I wrote, that the pupil had overtaken his master; it was a fact so obvious, he said, so blatant, he asserted, in short, something so undeniable it would've been preposterous to ignore, and I demanded he behold me, behold me, I screamed as I released my grip on Klein's collar, behold what has become of your learned understudy! And I pressed the blunt edge of my sword against his throat as a group of *Kleinians* approached, those odious upstarts, those nonentities, those vapid and tedious buffoons, and I myself stopped writing, stunned and nonplussed by Jacov's violence as well as the curious procurement of the sword, which I refrained from asking about, not to mention, in his words, the *extraordinary* escape from Klein's followers and hours later from Prague along with Sonja, who, he claimed, knew nothing of the incident. Yes, the *Kleinians* began to encircle me, Jacov continued, but I wished no further violence on my ex-master except for him to recognize he had chosen the wrong path, that is, the path *away* from melancholy and not *toward* melancholy, and that his ex-pupil had discovered the sacred path to the holy mountain beside the luminous stream that leads to melancholy, and although I later heard Klein had contacted the police, Jacov said and I wrote, we fled before the authorities could find us. Years before, however, with two dead parents and a fresh influx of Reinhardt tobacco money, Jacov retired to his estate in Belgrade, putting his research into melancholy on hiatus to investigate Emiliano Gomez Carrasquilla, something he had vigorously avoided out of deference to the man who had single-handedly rescued Jacov from the loneliness of the Harmsgradt Institute and Gymnasium with the small pamphlet *How Joy Saves Us,* and later with the larger philosophical works, which most European scholars, if they even paid attention, feigned indifference to or didn't take seriously, presupposing superiority over a lowly South American whose ideas they considered lowbrow and irrational; yet how, Jacov asked and I wrote, how could a serious mind not read *The Abstinence Sequence,* transposed later by Jacov as *The Fornication Sequence,* or *Pathways to Contentment,* also transposed by Jacov as *Boulevards of Grief,* and not appreciate the work of a first-rate mind wrestling with the notion of happiness, and thus melancholy? I was duty bound to learn what had become of this man, he said, whose works had begun to wane in the mid-1890s and eventually disappeared altogether by 1900. This dictated to me as a fire roared in the second Stuttgart castle study, and I felt a sense of bliss and belonging I'd never felt in the solitary village of my youth, and any time Jacov paused, and thus the dictation stopped, I gazed at my red-haired master, who had delivered me from mediocrity, whose pale legs with their sporadic copper hairs were sedentary one moment and ecstatic the next, in the same room, in fact, where years later we heard the distant howls of what at first we took to be a trapped animal or one of Ulrich's attack dogs that had escaped, but what Jacov ultimately recognized as Sonja, lost and wounded somewhere in the second Stuttgart castle. Enough dictation, Jacov roared, suddenly standing, sliding both feet inside his slippers, perceiving the screams as belonging to his lover and housekeeper and consort in so much of life, and even though their lovemaking had been on the decline, Jacov felt an affection and a loyalty and a warmth for Sonja that couldn't be put into words, for only days earlier he'd told me in a moment of rare sentiment, there are no words to explain how I feel for Sonja; she is simply one of my limbs, crucial to my survival, and when I lie to myself, he said, and thus the world, she is the first to notice and is never shy to tell me. The particular wing where Sonja had fallen was still under construction, a bizarre antechamber emanating from the back of the theater that jutted out just past the *meditation turret;* thus our difficulty in locating Sonja, fallen halfway through a hole in the floor, was an exercise in futility, poor Sonja, who was in no way hesitant about her feelings, cursing Jacov and his madness and the countless halls and slanting platforms and endless construction that had plagued all of us since we'd moved into the second Stuttgart castle, and if Sonja's curses grew louder, we rushed toward their source, and if fainter, we turned and attempted a new direction, tracking a bevy of profanities and cries whose tenuous source seemed both obscure and omnipotent. I checked the elevated courtyard next to the greenhouse and, finding nothing, entered the greenhouse itself, which, amid the silent snow of a bitter January, seemed surreal, replete with palms and orchids and vibrant azaleas while outside lay the frozen German countryside quiet as a coffin. Losing trace of Sonja's screams, I returned inside, first to the smoking room beside the second guest parlor attached to the third library, and again, finding nothing, I joined Jacov in the *Carrasquilla Wing*, where he was making lunatic circles listening to Sonja's insults, smiling dimly to himself, sniggering even, as if her abuse was an act of self-flagellation, and the more caustic and scathing her scorn the more he relished it, for he roared at God to punish him but to spare Sonja, punish me, he shouted, I'm the one guilty of pride and lacking the fortitude and endurance to find you through melancholy, and then Jacov resorted to the dead tongue of his dead twin, which always sent me into hysterics. I alerted Ulrich, who arrived in minutes, accompanied by a pair of immaculate Bordeaux mastiffs. Ulrich, whose poise and assurance emboldened me but infuriated Jacov, sniffed the air and clicked his tongue. Instinctively, he went to Sonja's apartment and seized a pair of her underwear, having his hounds sniff them before releasing them, lurching, across the estate. The dogs fanned out, finding corners and attics and belfries unseen since their inception, unearthing rooms and passages and even partitions unknown to any of us, for Jacov had hired and fired so many carpenters and architects and decorators, so many faces over the years, the faces of men Jacov had funded with Reinhardt tobacco money, many of them taking artistic liberties that betrayed both the contracts and the blueprints, that there existed countless clerestories and enfilades, not to mention hallways and foyers and porticos that, in theory, didn't exist but obviously did, salons veiled by trapdoors and false walls and bookshelves and even a kitchenette that hadn't witnessed a single human footstep until that desperate night. From the frequency and volume of their barks it was clear these Bordeaux mastiffs, recently adopted from a breeder in Ghent, had located Sonja with ease. They've located her with ease, Ulrich boasted. But we'd lost the dogs because they wouldn't return and lead us to Sonja, and now all three, the Bordeaux mastiffs and Sonja, wailed a song of singular anguish, the three of us searching for the three of them, and not for minutes but for hours, hours of Ulrich commanding the dogs to return and the Bordeaux mastiffs not only ignoring their master's calls but howling even louder along with Sonja, whose plaintive shrieks only strengthened our certainty that her injuries were grievous, for after calling Jacov a fucking scoundrel, a phony scholar, and a poor lover, she described her injuries as grievous. Two greyhounds, charged with protecting the outdoor grounds, were brought inside to join the cause; within minutes their barks joined the chorus, and, like their brethren, the Bordeaux mastiffs, they refused to return. Are they falling into a black hole? Jacov cursed, stamping the marble floor in his slippers. For the next two hours the Bordeaux mastiffs, escorted by the greyhounds and Sonja, wailed in concert, punctuated by Sonja's insults, her calling Jacov a bastard, a wretch, and a phony intellectual among other things much worse, but eventually Sonja grew silent, and it was her silence most of all that made us worry, and Jacov attempted to buoy her spirits, encouraging her to hold on to life. Hold on to life, he cried, cling to hope, he shouted, and Ulrich, now with a fifth pair of Sonja's panties, suggested releasing a pair of lean and graceful Eurohounds recently purchased from a broker in Düsseldorf, which Jacov bluntly refused, convinced a black hole or, at the very least, another dimension had unsealed itself on his estate, for he had studied alternate dimensions and parallel universes in his twenties, a short phase but a phase of intense study nonetheless, and this had all the hallmarks of a hole opening, he confirmed, of a new universe presenting itself, and only the hounds' and Sonja's dogged yearning to hold fast to this world was keeping them, clinging, to our dimension. It was just before dawn when Jacov suddenly recalled the alcove he'd insisted be built amid the joie de vivre of a recent cocaine binge, an alcove only half-finished and difficult to access but that Jacov swore he could find. The alcove sat behind the theater, beside a small niche above an unfinished fitting room in an obscure and isolated corridor of the castle, where an outlandish fresco of Jacov atop a raven-hued stallion adorned the wall, the painting an exercise in extravagance with the subject, Jacov, of course, in stark relief from the surrounding landscape: a world of precipitous cliffs, heartache, and oblivion; lightning illuminated the sky; insipid pastures, not unlike the dreaded pastures of Croatia, stood behind my master's likeness, heavy streaks of ashen gray and bitter plum, and one couldn't help but regard the painting and discern a world vanquished of hope. Broaching the niche, the noise of the barks instantly grew, and Ulrich, leading the charge with candles, climbed over a half-finished wall past a plethora of construction materials to find an unconscious Sonja in a pool of blood so dense we assumed she had died, for poor Sonja had not only fallen through the floor, but her left leg had been impaled on the other side as well, that is, beneath her, by a rod of steel, and though there must have been an inconceivable abundance of blood below, that is, on the first floor, there was an astounding amount surrounding her torso too, and this made me queasy, for the human body and its myriad components has never agreed with me, as there is something feeble and infirm in its elemental crudity, the way the flesh falls so easily ill and grows so quickly old, not to mention the diseases shrouded within, unseen, that are practically lying in wait, so much so that a single healthy day on earth seems almost a miracle in and of itself, and then Jacov returned me to the scene with his blood-curdling howl, because the spectacle before us was undeniably gruesome yet, seconds later, I observed the most tender supplication as Jacov pressed Sonja's head against his breast, adorning her face with fervent kisses, and all the while Ulrich was sizing up the situation, the loss of blood, the injury itself, and swiftly he got to work making a tourniquet from his shirt, grabbing a saw, and doing the unthinkable act that ultimately saved her, and later, that is, after her return from the Stuttgart hospital, the three of us, meaning Jacov, Ulrich, and myself, quickly learned that the loss of a limb doesn't merely alter the person but also presents an entirely *new* person. The Sonja returned from the Stuttgart hospital with an oak leg was, in theory, the same Sonja we'd always known, perhaps a Sonja slightly altered or badly maimed or even peg-legged, but this wasn't the case at all, for she returned wholly rearranged, a Sonja with an entirely different set of beliefs and outlooks on life, for her expressions and mannerisms, her attitude and soul, had been marked by that night, by the hours we spent clamoring and searching and cursing Ulrich's beloved hounds, and Jacov imagined Sonja facing her own annihilation, for he later told me, I imagine her facing her own annihilation, and once I reflect on this, he said, on my sweet, radiant Sonja facing her own annihilation, I obsess, that is, I banish all other thoughts, and I torment myself imagining the agony of that interminable night, of her knowing, even as we called out, that intrepid death was standing close by, tapping its fingers. Sonja's leg, or lack thereof, made Jacov immensely uncomfortable, and, noticing this, Sonja made sure to bring extra attention to the leg, or lack thereof, striking a match across the prosthetic limb to light a cigarette or scratching it with her nails and blaming a phantom itch, so that the more uncomfortable Jacov became with the leg, or lack thereof, the more frequently Sonja scratched it or unfastened it or tapped it on the marble floor, in short, the more she intentionally brought attention to the wooden leg, and whether it was a case of the leg, or lack thereof, or the guilt associated with the leg, or lack thereof, that agitated Jacov most, it was never said, yet the change in Sonja was absolute, for it wasn't a case of Jacov or myself or Ulrich seeing Sonja in a new light but of Sonja having returned from the Stuttgart hospital wholly transformed, for she was without question an entirely different woman, one who laughed at things the earlier, two-legged Sonja would not have found the least bit charming, and her eyes invited darker hues while containing an almost palpable absence of light, and though the beauty of her face was still irrefutable with its lustrous pallor and pale radiance, there existed the supple tracks of nameless terrors, footprints left by the monsters who visited each night. Her voice had changed octaves too, lower and throatier, and bitterness doesn't give justice to the shadows that now crossed her brow, for in her

eyes plans were being made, theories drawn, and if she didn't
blame Jacov, which she insisted she didn't, she blamed fate itself,
a fate she would curse and scorn and abhor for the rest of her
days, and I saw other, smaller changes, her taste in poetry, for
instance, and one afternoon I found her tossing her collection
of Lake Poets into the fire, the first and second editions of
Wordsworth and Coleridge replete with painstaking marginalia reduced first to ashes then smoke that drifted through the
chimney and across the second Stuttgart castle to slowly dissipate over the meadows of greater Stuttgart itself. I, of course,
was not around on Sonja's return, for that tragic night had also
left its mark on me, and I checked myself into a clinic in
Degerloch, a short distance from the estate, for I had diagnosed
myself with a nervous disorder that had never been documented,
wholly original, the first of its kind, and thus, having no name,
I presented to the doctors a real dilemma, though its lack of a
name didn't make it any less real, something a few of the nurses
seemed only too happy to suggest, but no, it was acute, more
palpable than a plum in one's palm, because the trauma and
violence of that night was utterly lucid: the recollection of Sonja
regaining consciousness, the grim resonance of Ulrich sawing
into her leg, the spasm of pain and recognition of what was
occurring, the fawn-like trembling in her eyes, the belt Ulrich
made her bite down on, the way Jacov paced in delirious circles
reciting mantras and Zen koans instead of going for help; we
are all lost, he shouted, rubbing his Buddhist beads, we are all

lost, he wailed in agony, contradicting, in fact, the Diamond Sutra tong-len mantra he kept reciting, and I was uncertain if they were truly Tibetan mantras or his dead sister's tongue, for both sounded viscous and infernal; I gazed in horror as Jacov pleaded with celestial realms and beseeched the cosmos, pulling at the red strands of hair that stuck out, unkempt, across the sides of his head. We are all lost, he raved, lost to this rapacious death that surrounds us, a death that's never sated, never-ending and infernal, a death panting like these goddamn mutts, and Jacov threw a blood-soaked slipper in the direction of the greyhounds. All of it was too much. Yes, my nerves were in disarray, and even the doctors weren't sure what to make of me, though they insisted I was in fine health, perfect health, *almost enviable health,* said Dr. Gerthoffer, except for, of course, my nerves, which could use a bit of a holiday, a reprieve from Jacov and the second Stuttgart castle, which over the years had become notorious among the Stuttgart city limits and farther, for the endless construction gave the impression to any tourist or sightseer or ignorant fool, in short, a person who knew nothing about anything, of being haphazard and reckless, the enterprise of an obvious lunatic, and these false beliefs gave rise to rumors of cult rituals and divination, all sorts of dubious projects not excluding satanic ceremonies, and admittedly my constant errands to procure cocaine from doctors and lately Stuttgart street goons didn't bode well, yet I was convinced the rumors were given life by the architects and landscapers themselves, for it's well known that architects and landscapers are shameless gossips and defamers, thus the legions that Jacov had fired had scores to settle, and Dr. Gerthoffer, bending to meet my eyes, queried in the most sober of tones, *what goes on in there, anyway?* My stay in Degerloch was brief, for the doctor's failure to find anything, from a minute diagnosis to anything hinting vaguely at an affliction of a more serious caliber, coupled with their insistence on my vigorous constitution, which only convinced me more of my ill health, so that the more they maintained my staunch health, the more certain I was of approaching death, struck me as inept or dishonest, both being unacceptable, and so I returned to the second Stuttgart castle, where at least my ailments were taken with a certain degree of gravity. Thus I recouped. And thus a period of adjustment followed, mostly with Jacov and I listening from upstairs to the sound of Sonja's wooden leg below, its cadence telling us the degree of her ill mood as well as alerting us to which room she was now residing in, limping to the kitchen to stir a stew or perhaps hobbling through the various libraries to collect and contain the dust Jacov was so fanatical about and which he'd just finished dictating a portfolio's worth of theories on; *dust, dust, dust,* he would mutter between the thumps of Sonja's wooden limb, for she vehemently refused to muffle the sounds by adorning her prosthetic with either sock or slipper, not for anyone's benefit, and the ceaseless knocking, the afflicted cadence, had driven Jacov and me to the second floor, where we'd become hostages in some macabre performance authored by a peg-legged director whose final act had yet to be written. Jacov insisted Sonja rest, as she was his friend and lover and lifelong guest, and besides, he said, the second Stuttgart castle was too immense, too daunting and abstract, for just a single housekeeper, *especially a housekeeper with one leg,* he muttered under his breath, since the two of us shared an intrinsic fear that a tempest was building, an outburst long unheeded, and the longer we waited for Sonja's eruption the worse it would be, and I fear her calm more than her rage, Jacov confessed, for when she's calm, which, let's admit it, is her constant state, it means the rage is still building, the anger not having yet found its zenith, and who knows what that will look like or what form it will take? Yet Sonja refused to stop, insisting the work suited her temper, and I believe part of Jacov relished the solitude, the three of us and an occasional appearance from Ulrich, if he wasn't in the Ardennes or the Black Forest trapping and collecting mongrels, and besides, Jacov said, whatever Sonja isn't able to clean doesn't need cleaning; the dust brings me undeniable pleasure, he said, the beveled glass with its layers of grime, he said, and the furniture that languishes from disuse, all of it is infinitely agreeable; thus, we hid upstairs as Sonja hobbled from room to room, and Jacov indulged in larger and more frequent helpings of cocaine, which he routinely maintained, assisted him in forming the synthesis for studying and dictating the highs and lows and middles of melancholy. And so it wasn't long before Jacov was reminded of his life's work, primarily through meditation and cocaine or through cocaine and meditation, the order being immaterial, and he soon became fixated with the idea of traveling to South America and finding Emiliano Gomez Carrasquilla himself, for an article had appeared in a rather small and insignificant scholarly journal reminding Jacov of Carrasquilla, an article speculating on Carrasquilla's disappearance in 1901, remarking on Carrasquilla's refusal to ever write again after his last book, *Finding Bliss*, inverted later by Jacov as *Locating Despair*, was published. The article described Carrasquilla's work in rather unflattering terms, calling him second-rate and sophomoric and rather dull, focusing more on Carrasquilla's strange and nomadic life, finding his background worthier of attention than a single word he'd ever written, yet the article nonetheless reminded Jacov of having abandoned his master. I've abandoned my master, he said one afternoon as we followed the sound of Sonja's leg beneath us, from the second sitting room to the main kitchen, where, from the sounds of it, she was in a foul temper. I wasted so much time, Jacov confessed, falling under the spell of Klein, becoming a *Kleinian*, just as I would become and later renounce being a Tolstoyan; in any case, I wasted so much time looking at myself for the answers instead of looking for Carrasquilla, and then Jacov sniffed several lines of cocaine before lamenting not visiting the source. I never considered visiting the source, he said, either from fear or cowardice, although the reason is beside the point, for the result is the same in that I simply refused to act on the single thing that has been calling me since the discovery of Carrasquilla, which is my meeting face-to-face with Carrasquilla, because Carrasquilla has been calling me all along, and only direct contact with Carrasquilla will advance my work on melancholy and thus allow me to complete my life's work, since Carrasquilla is the connection I need and the connection I've always needed to find the path to authentic melancholy, and now Carrasquilla is living in the jungle, San Rafael if I recall, older than age itself, most likely lost and aimless and in need of our help; so stand up, Jacov ordered, and I looked into his eyes, which were trembling and bloodshot. The Uruguayans had loaded the mules, and everyone, I realized, was waiting for me to stand, to finally walk after a week of being carried by stretcher, and perhaps I was cured, and perhaps my fever had abated, but what matter? Standing frightened me. Walking frightened me. Everything in the world frightened me, and yet all it took was Jacov, in a moment of rare composure, to kneel beside me and tell me his life's work had only come this far because of me; it has only survived this far, he said, because of you, and it will only continue until it's complete because of you, for you, he said, are my loyal servant and pupil and factotum, and if not the agency necessary for my life's work, you are at the very least the buttress or support or the *footing* necessary for my life's work, and your weak constitution is compensated in full by your devotion, and I began to cry as he whispered in my ear stronger, more robust words of encouragement, words that sent bolts of electricity through my limbs so that when I stood I felt, if not reborn, partially renewed, and no matter the disease or climate or the threat of indigenous clans, none of it would impinge on our finding Carrasquilla and thus pure, unadulterated melancholy, and I hadn't seen Jacov so lucid, so *returned* to his former self in ages, and he was the father and friend I'd never had, and my love for him was unfathomable and bottomless, it permeated everything, and so I finally stood and we continued our trek, with Ulrich fixated on San Rafael and the telegraph and Jacov fixated on either returning to Montevideo for cocaine or finding Carrasquilla, whichever came first, and me fixated on Jacov's happiness, which, in essence, was either returning to Montevideo for cocaine or finding Carrasquilla, who could be anywhere in the Gualeguaychú forest, and only five Uruguayan guides remained in our party as well as that cursed linguist, Javier, who'd been banished from speaking altogether, and the pack mules too, whose ribs pushed through their gaunt flanks like an accordion's bellows and all of us covered in mud, resembling some lost tribe from the ends of the earth, a sort of hallucination; we walked all morning as the sun flickered through the canopy and our shadows danced, through dense scrubland teeming with the Yaro, and Ulrich confessed his unwavering belief that we were being followed by the Yaro, had likely been followed by the Yaro for days, perhaps longer, and if his coordinates were correct, we were walking straight through the middle of Yaro territory, a tribe intent on our deaths since that absurd trade months before, and if only I had my beloved attack dogs with me, said Ulrich, and I hadn't before seen Ulrich so unnerved, an emotion I believed him incapable of having. Gradually the path sloped, and this slope encouraged Ulrich, who whispered, this slope is encouraging, for I'm certain it's the selfsame slope we passed the day before stumbling upon San Rafael the first time. But I wasn't concerned anymore with what encouraged Ulrich, for I had observed his slippery soul and how quickly he would betray our master to return to civilization, and thus I concerned myself solely with my master's state of mind and our advance toward Montevideo for cocaine or perhaps finding Carrasquilla, whichever came first, for Jacov's words had not only rejuvenated me but had also caused me to reassert my allegiance, an allegiance I hadn't felt since escaping the swaying nightmare of the *SS Unerschrocken,* a journey that would've tested the resolves of the strongest men. Jacov had caressed my soul when I'd needed it most, and I was reminded why I loved every fiber of this man, from his saintlike passion to the pasty hillock of his exuberant paunch, and I forgave him for everything, from his self-absorption to all his middling promiscuities, for isn't genius forever afflicted by the crudity of bad choices? I loved Jacov, and the only way to express this love was to continue searching for Emiliano Gomez Carrasquilla, the prophet he'd studied and analyzed as a young man in Belgrade, even traveling to Cologne to meet Elsa Weber,

Carrasquilla's German translator, in person, to find out what had become of his spirit guide and wisdom teacher. Elsa Weber, a woman whose haunting intelligence and eggshell skin had seduced Jacov, who, in turn, had tried to seduce Weber and failed. I tried to seduce Elsa Weber, he said, and failed; although there was a strong physical attraction between us, this was undeniable, she was annoyed by my reading or, according to her, my *misreading* of Carrasquilla's books. I traveled to Cologne and spoke to Elsa Weber, Jacov dictated to me on a sultry summer day in Stuttgart with the windows open and the scent of cut grass drifting through the study; I spoke to her of the beauty and grace of true melancholy, but after three days of speaking to her about the beauty and grace of true melancholy, three days wherein I found myself berating Elsa Weber for her lack of understanding about the beauty and grace of true melancholy, I grew fed up, for much like Otto Klein, Elsa Weber took philosophy and theology and the sciences *literally;* thus, she believed in taking Carrasquilla's works *literally,* hence she translated his works *literally,* and I told her that if I took Carrasquilla's writings at face value, that is, literally, he would be the biggest fool and counterfeit to have ever lived, and I an even bigger fool and counterfeit for reading him, for who, I asked her, spends their intellectual career dedicated to studying happiness? A child? I asked. A mentally unstable half-wit? I demanded. No, I told her, Emiliano Gomez Carrasquilla is a philosophical humorist, the most unique of thinkers in that solitary arena, solitary because in the whole of human history there's so far only been one philosophical humorist and that is Carrasquilla, and one doesn't study happiness and joy and contentment at the *dawn* of one's intellectual career, for happiness and joy and contentment are the *destination* of one's intellectual career, and not until one has traveled the dark and menacing paths of pathos, the bramble-infested corridors of anguish, does one learn that *happiness* and *melancholy* are two words for the same thing. And I instructed Elsa Weber in her small apartment that almost overlooked the Rhine that melancholy was the highest and most esteemed emotion a human soul was capable of feeling, and I elucidated for Elsa Weber in her tiny flat that could barely house a gnat or a mouse let alone a human being that Carrasquilla's works are a response to those indolent, superficial intellectuals who believe the living of life is so much confectionary. No, I told Elsa Weber, finally tying her to a chair with rope inside her apartment that afforded only the most narrow glimpse of the Rhine, not to torture or imprison, no, but to constrain her so that she'd simply listen to reason, so that she'd understand that Carrasquilla, like myself, had suffered a horrible tragedy, likely at a very young age, and I went on to tell Elsa Weber about the loss of my twin and the death of our language and the outcasts we were in that blasphemous hole Knin, which was both a tragedy and a gift, for with Vita's death I beheld the sadness inherent in life, a sadness that expands like vapor and is thus uncontained, reaching every unchartered recess of the soul, a sadness one discerns if, like me, one's eyes are open, a sadness that becomes inextricable from one's very existence, and this elevated me, for I realized that life carries only fleeting promises and very little hope except through the understanding of pathos, and Emiliano Gomez Carrasquilla also saw this, for there exists, he recalled and I wrote, a palpable agony that permeates and infuses all of Carrasquilla's books, and Elsa Weber, restrained to a chair in her flat, which contained the most meager view of the Rhine, a view like a kick in the stomach, a view that merely teased the eye, a perpetual torture no doubt because of its paltry perspective of the Rhine, for the Rhine is a splendid and robust river that courses through Cologne like a bent femur, Jacov said and I wrote, and to be given a sliver of the Rhine but not an entire view of the Rhine is worse than being blind to the Rhine altogether, to be ignorant of the Rhine's existence, for imagine being so close to such an esteemed waterway as the Rhine, so near to a beloved estuary one can almost dive in, only to be shut out because of the idiocy of the architect or the greed of the landlord or perhaps both, and part of me wanted desperately to ask what she paid for that disgusting dump of a flat, but I couldn't digress, for my trip and my focus and my design was for one thing, he said and I wrote, and that was to discover the fate of Emiliano Gomez Carrasquilla. So, I told Elsa Weber, if you can't see Carrasquilla's works for the satires they are, you're incapable of seeing the man you've translated, the philosophical burlesque that makes his works wholly original, and I see little hope for you, and at this point, with the sun having set, Elsa Weber seemed lethargic, for she had grown tired from the restraints and was asking, pleading in fact, for water, and so I gave her two glasses, and then I rummaged through her horribly cramped flat in Cologne for any correspondence she may have had with the great South American oracle, and finding nothing besides transcripts and textbooks and tiny figurines of porcelain rabbits that she collected, I finally lay down and slept, and the next morning, after a rather grievous slumber in her bed, which mimicked her apartment in that they were both abominable, I made us both cups of tea and told her I wanted to know *everything* about Carrasquilla, and Elsa Weber, a strawberry blond in her late thirties with green eyes, eggshell skin, and diminutive lips that suggested only one thing, finally ceded, and though I had lost respect for Elsa Weber's work as a translator and no longer saw Elsa Weber as a person of the rarest intellect, she knew things, and for the next two days I inquired on countless subjects, focusing, of course, on how she had received Carrasquilla's transcripts in the first place, the location of his German publishers, the notes and suggestions Carrasquilla invariably gave her, and last, but most important, why he had stopped writing, but actually not last, next to last, for what I most wanted to know was where he, he being Carrasquilla, now lived, and Elsa Weber, with the ropes around her wrists and ankles loosened for relief, explained that Carrasquilla's deep religious awakening had forced the abdication of writing for a sacred or spiritual or sublime calling, because with each successive book he had felt *the creeping fingers of hypocrisy snatching at him,* an expression she hadn't forgotten, written, she explained, in the only letter she had ever received from Carrasquilla, in which Carrasquilla thanked Elsa Weber for her faithful translations and went on to say he felt compelled to live a *physical* life of joy instead of a life writing about *practicing* joy and I observed Elsa Weber's green eyes, Jacov said and I wrote, as she explained the little she remembered from that long-ago letter, how Carrasquilla had wanted to live a life at peace with the land, to abandon thought en masse, to discard intellectualism altogether, and in this single letter he briefly mentioned his desire to leave the scrub and underbrush of Uruguay, to go west through the Gualeguaychú forest; perhaps he'd mentioned a village, San Luís or San Miguel or perhaps San Rafael, although she wasn't sure of its exact name or even which country since the letter had been written years before and put inside a desk to be forgotten and eventually thrown away, and there was no discussion or climax or turmoil when he retired, she said, for the translation of his works into German was almost a fluke, purely happenstance, merely the obsession of the publishers, two old eccentrics, veterans of the Seven Weeks' War, long since dead, and my translations of his works into German were something that made not even the slightest ripple in the academic or intellectual community, she continued, and I, being only a student when I began the project, eventually forgot about all of his work since I had to make my way in the world. As for being chosen to translate Carrasquilla, Elsa Weber explained, it wasn't a case of being chosen but rather nominating oneself since no one was interested in the translation of this South American, I don't know what you'd call him, *enigma* or *zero;* in any case, a *nobody* to Germans and South Americans alike. But I was fluent, she explained, both in reading and writing Spanish since Spanish was spoken in my home as a child, my mother having grown up in Granada, and by chance, I glimpsed an advertisement in some minor journal querying the services of a translator and I replied, that is, I said yes, for you see I had wanted to become a translator, although, she admitted, I've since given up translation, and I now work in the library off Lindenthalgürtel, but his books were fully disregarded and later pulped, she told Jacov and I wrote, and even the publishers, she told Jacov, are dead and defunct, and how you came upon them in Belgrade, she began to say, but before she could finish Jacov interrupted her to point out that he'd come upon the works of Carrasquilla strictly by fate, fate he howled, fate he spat as he paced in circles around Elsa Weber in that shithole of a flat, a circle being the only pattern or shape or path the limited space allowed, and fate, he emphasized to a very startled Elsa Weber, was his second-favorite word in any spoken or written language after the most illustrious and noble and enchanting word, which was, of course, *melancholy.* In his one letter Carrasquilla explained to Elsa Weber how he yearned to live a monastic life, a life free from the burdens and exhaustions of writing, free from the pains of not only writing but of *thinking* and then *writing,* which are two entirely different acts, thinking being one and writing being the other, but acts that undoubtedly depend on one another since one doesn't happen without the other, and many people believe writing is a single act, he'd written in his one letter to Elsa Weber, an exercise in and of itself, but it's not that at all, it's three or four, perhaps six different acts, because there's the idea of course and then one needs the words to carry that idea because without the words the idea simply sinks or suffocates; in short, it dies, but no one mentions the discipline or the self-motivation and self-belief nor the energy and agony of having to sit and write about what, at least for him, was essentially life, but while doing this you're not only avoiding life, he'd written, you're oblivious to life, blind to life, it's perhaps the negation of life itself, and in a sense writing is a form of death and what's more, he'd written to Elsa Weber, my soul is crying for silence, to put an end to the avalanche of words, that's the exact word he used, said Elsa Weber, *avalanche.* And the more she talked of this single letter she'd received and ultimately thrown away, the more Jacov wanted to read it and thus the more upset he became, and Elsa Weber summarized what she remembered of Carrasquilla's letter, which was simply that Carrasquilla had come to the conclusion that writing itself was an illness, one he desired to cure himself of by turning away, by traveling into the interior of this seemingly endless continent, and even though his works would later influence Rubén Darío and Horacio Quiroga and a small litany of modernists, how was he to know? And Jacov gazed past the window to a view that *almost* gave a person a glimpse of the Rhine but in reality gave a person only the *promise* of the Rhine, the sounds and the scents of the Rhine but never the Rhine itself, never that breathtaking and opulent waterway, for Elsa Weber's lone window simply looked across the alley toward a neighboring tenement, a view that was more like a *nonview* in that the more one looked, the more one realized how little they saw, and a person would have to lean their body at a ninety-degree angle to see even the thinnest sliver of the Rhine, a sliver like an insult, a sliver like a joke at one's expense, and if this box, he said, this crappy hole, he stammered, this absurd dwelling is what modern cities are becoming, then he truly loathed and rejected the impending catastrophe of civilization, and what a word that was, he seethed, for there was nothing civil about it at all, and Elsa Weber, tied to a chair in a flat Jacov wouldn't wish on Otto Klein himself, a flat like a closet or a shoe box but a shoe box meant to hold the shoes of children or dwarfs and certainly not shoes meant for full, regular-sized adults, continued to explain that hardly anyone read or discussed or cared about Carrasquilla's works, no one, in fact, she added, not a single human, except perhaps as an obscure footnote or a name used as the butt of some joke, but a highly specific joke.

No one was the slightest bit familiar with Carrasquilla's name, and I did the work, she said, that is, the translations, for philanthropic reasons, as well as for my own edification, but essentially for charity while taking my degree, never making a single cent, and judging from her infinitesimal apartment, Jacov said, translation paid about as well as working in the library, and what a good idea it was to inherit Reinhardt tobacco money, he reflected, and more people should do the same, as it gives one the time and ease to reflect on life's plethora of anxieties. Elsa Weber told Jacov that no one, besides the now-defunct publishers, had ever mentioned Carrasquilla's name to her, and she had quite perfectly forgotten about him as if he'd never existed or was one of those specters from a childhood dream that returns after decades, suddenly and irrationally, and you're reminded of the dream, a ridiculous fantasy, a delusion that would've never occurred if it hadn't reared its head once again; yes, forgotten about him utterly and completely until Jacov had appeared in her hall outside what Jacov assumed was the most minuscule apartment in human history, and Emiliano Gomez Carrasquilla, she concluded, has had no influence in the intellectual world, and this sentence shook Jacov to his core, this sentence was enough to make Jacov flee Elsa Weber's microscopic slum without looking back, to escape Cologne and retreat, by train, to the Holstooraf Sanatorium and Spa, to recover and reconvene, to collect himself, never fully convinced he'd ever untied Elsa Weber from that chair in her cesspool of a flat, and soon thereafter, meaning three weeks later, Jacov found solace at the Holstooraf Sanatorium and Spa, both in my friendship and by thrusting his loins against Sonja's loins in the broom closet, the hedge maze, the attic of the TB ward, behind the topiaries, and, to hear Jacov tell it, many other locations, and though I don't know which came first, all of it, the order of events, the quiet wonder of life unfolding, had me believing in fate as well, for how else had the three of us met and become intimate friends and, consequently, found ourselves living in the first Stuttgart castle beside the Möllers and their odious orchard? And I considered fate as we tramped in silence through the never-ending fog, the buttocks of Javier's mule the only thing I could make out, because fog removes the dimensions of the world and gives equal proportions to every object, casting a veneer on existence in which the consequences are vague and counterfeit, and suddenly Ulrich was beside me with the gravest of expressions, urging me to stop walking. Stop walking, he whispered, and then he said the same to Javier, and slowly he disappeared through the fog to tell each in our party to do the same, that is, to stop walking, and while they're at it to shut their mouths too, and I wasn't one to worry much about being attacked, as I already had enough on my mind, what with my bad ankle and the perpetual threats of the *phantom headaches*, but something in Ulrich's expression brought me back to the night of Sonja's amputation and even further back to the Tula station platform, the expression Ulrich wore the moment he located us, that is, Jacov and myself, and I understood now that Ulrich wore that expression only on the most terrible and grave occasions, not even occasions but *crises*, and that we were, indeed, on the verge of being attacked or perhaps already under attack, for with that damnable fog, who could tell what was taking place inches away? It could well be under way *now*, for I was unversed in the violence of the physical world, having enough to attend to with my various maladies, entire seasons spent in bed as I anguished over the next undiagnosed epidemic, crouching in the corner and biding its time or circling my bed; no, I knew little of battles except the invasions waged by the human body on itself, and the next moment Ulrich emerged through the fog, instructing me to lie on the ground. We're surrounded, he said, and I never thought to ask what we were surrounded *by*, for there hadn't been a single occasion on this continent that we weren't surrounded by something vile and impenetrable, something unnamable but all the worse for having no name, something following and pressing against us, suffocating us, seeking to deliver fever and death, only this time we were surrounded by the Yaro, and they had been following us for weeks, perhaps months, Ulrich managed to say, Yaro who were armed and intrepid, who had awoken that morning with the sole intention of killing us, and I cursed our ignorance, our half-hearted guides, our ineffectual translator, who lacked the discretion and good sense to speak his native tongue without incident. Follow me toward the river, Ulrich instructed in a whisper, and all of us on our stomachs now followed Ulrich through the underbrush, and soon we were dragging ourselves across the mud toward the sound of the water, and I was certain the trees around us had fluttered, and I waited for the darts or the arrows or the gunshots to start, and I was third behind Ulrich, our troop now a segmented snake but a snake unaccustomed to traveling on its stomach, suddenly aware of its own impending extinction, and I yearned to turn and see the red flames of Jacov's hair glowing through the fog, but I kept my face on the wet earth as we shimmied and floundered, totally unnatural maneuvers for bipeds, animals wistfully aware of the tragedy upon them, and we'd abandoned our mules and our supplies without a thought, for things in the jungle turned grave in a second, not even a second but the merciless time between seconds, the time with no name because it's so short and which divides one second from the one that follows, and I regarded the lunacy of our expedition, the incompetence of our translator, the lack of a precise direction, for we had crossed an ocean and landed on a continent with no more than a name, Emiliano Gomez Carrasquilla, and a place, San Rafael, and I also considered our idiot circles and our half-witted retreats and our never truly knowing if we were coming or going, whether we had ever left the Gualeguaychú forest, if we had remained in Uruguay or breeched Argentina or even Brazil, and suddenly I thought of Sonja and the depth of her soul, Sonja, who told us when we left that we were idiots, idiots for leaving but, more important, idiots because we were men and it was in our natures and thus it couldn't be helped, this said at the foot of the second Stuttgart castle as we departed, spoken not with malice or rancor but with pity, which is always worse, for she pitied us and our designs as if she knew something we were incapable of understanding. Sonja never tried to prevent us from leaving, she simply accepted our journey as something we couldn't help but indulge in, and as I pulled my body along the tall grass, I recalled the insistence with which Sonja seized her papers and books as her leg was getting removed, literally sawed off; she glared with predatory eyes at the attic space in which she had clearly spent thousands of hours, a crawl space designed to suit her needs, principally reading and writing, for I remember turning to see the stacks of papers and notes and the tottering bookshelf containing her beloved poets and even a small black-and-white photograph of Alva Belmont and a sketch of Annette von Droste-Hülshoff nailed to the wall, poets and suffragettes, for this obscure space, this half-forgotten wing of the second Stuttgart castle, was Sonja's solace, the place in which she hid herself away to write and perhaps translate, and I remember how she insisted her work be retrieved on her return from the hospital, all her books and papers accounted for, since Sonja contained depths Jacov and myself hadn't ever bothered to consider, and she hadn't withdrawn and receded to be *away* from us but rather to be *alone* with her thoughts, and in that tiny attic bursting with endless stacks of books, hidden and hoarded and cherished, I realized Sonja saw books and words the same as she saw making love, received the same voluptuous pleasure from touch as she did the words used to describe touch, for she was a sensualist and thus no delineation existed between the flesh of a man and the lines of a poem, both containing beating hearts and vital organs and viscera, all worthy of being preserved and protected, and if anyone's soul coincided with Carrasquilla's it was Sonja's, for both desired nothing more than the solitude of one's thoughts, her hidden crawl space beautifully converted into a literary salon for one, and Sonja, like so many of us, perhaps all of us, was born in the wrong place and time, and she once confessed that she'd written five volumes of poetry, all unpublished, for this is what happens when we are born into false destinies, and for us it was too late, death had arrived, but for Sonja, immersed in the second Stuttgart castle, busy collecting dust or translating poems and watching the fifth and final wing of the second Stuttgart castle reach completion, there was still a future. Meanwhile, we were crawling on our stomachs, on the verge of being murdered, and I heard the tramping of feet in the tall grass, and how capricious and irrational death is, for it's always advancing but never in the way one expects. I saw an arrow strike the mud beside me, heard a thin, whistling sound, steady and innocuous, not unlike a mosquito hovering beside one's ear, and then darts all around, raining upon us, and the screams of Javier in his ridiculous accent so even in death I found it hard to sympathize for him, and I slithered my body past his, faster through the mud, an enfilade of arrows hissing through the air, arrows likely dipped in poisonous curare, and coupled now with the howls of the Yaro and the shrieks of our party, and where was Jacov or, more important, how could Jacov conceivably crawl, encumbered as he was with the *Origin Books* pressed against his belly, the most precious and priceless objects on earth, said Jacov, the most audacious and distilled statement on human nature, said Jacov, the most original formulation of our capacities, added Jacov, and thus I was to protect the *Origin Books* at all costs. If I perish, he'd instructed me no less than the day before, if a catastrophe befalls me, you must bring them back to Europe, for the *Origin Books* are the world's salvation and the answer to the question no one has bothered to ask, and though, he'd added, they are written in my and dear Vita's tongue, there is a code, a key I've made to decipher the books, except an argument broke out between Javier and a guide over the proper technique for grilling bushmeat so that the cipher, the code, the key for the *Origin Books* was, like the ideas and theories themselves, wholly inside Jacov's brain, never divulged, and I hadn't the chance nor sense to press Jacov on its whereabouts, busy as I was with my fever and other catalogue of complaints. I crawled until the grass receded and found myself on the edge of the bank, and by good fortune it had begun to rain, for this hampered visibility, although these Indians were undaunted, and I squeezed beside Ulrich, waiting for the others, and Ulrich wore the strangest expression I'd ever seen until I realized it was the expression of someone who had taken several arrows in the back, arrows that now protruded through his chest and guts. Ulrich made a brave face as he tried to pull them out, but there were too many, no less than six that I counted, and I cried in soft gasps as the blood spread across his shirt in gushes so thick, so prodigious and unrelenting, that when I looked again he had expired, and Ulrich was no more, no more collecting outlandish rents from countless properties, no more catching and training attack dogs across Europe, and I gazed at the prominent scar along his forehead, a scar whose source would always remain a mystery, and I recalled his sudden appearance on the Tula station platform like a headhunter, a villain, and how our bond had begun in what seemed the long-remote past, all of it a fable or a dream, for what is the past but a collective dream shared by the dream's characters? Nearby came the cries of our guides, and inside them I tried to locate Jacov's but found nothing, and in this chaos I asked myself, should I turn and go back for my master or jump into the rising river or perhaps lie facedown in the mud and feign death? I, of course, decided on the last, even smearing Ulrich's blood on my clothes for good measure, and I pressed my face into the mud, wanting only to crawl deeper inside the womb of the earth. And thus time passed, rain fell, and the cries of my cohorts dwindled; later I felt the footsteps of the tribe, who came to examine their work and spoke in a tongue that reminded me of Jacov and Vita's in that it was the dialect of death, and they simply kicked our bodies, that is, Ulrich's and mine, with disinterest and soon thereafter disappeared through the rain. At nightfall I turned to see the canopy above, the moonlight quivering through the trees. The rain had abated, and gathering my wits, I turned and crawled through the grass, passing the expired bodies of the party, Javier and the Uruguayans, the mules gone, taken most likely, and I crawled faster, looking for my dear master until I came upon an expanse of shorter grass and flat earth. I was on the verge of abandoning my crawl to stand when my head knocked into Jacov's. He lay on his back, the bulge of the *Origin Books* rising toward the sky accompanied by the heads of two arrows that seemed to have been propelled straight from the earth itself. His eyes were closed but he was breathing, and I said his name and in dull recognition his head turned as he began to unbutton his shirt, and I commenced weeping, for I knew he was bequeathing me the *Origin Books*, the realization of his imminent death apparent to both of us, and *how*, I asked myself, how, out of everyone, had I survived? Jacov's thoughts were in a similar vein, for he smiled and muttered, how, how are *you* alive, you with your fevers and headaches and your goddamn ankle? I shook my head, for I had no ready answer. Perhaps I had escaped death, I said, because I feared it the most, and Jacov smiled and unfastened three more buttons, neither one of us lucid enough to consider the most pressing issue, that of the code or key necessary to translate his masterwork, for if the *Origin Books* were written, as Jacov claimed, in the singular tongue of his and his dead sister's invention, how would I unravel it? Before the subject could be broached however, Jacov had stopped breathing forever, his hand on the fifth button, and I wept, for I had lived and he had not, and death, so serene and uneventful, so unlike what one reads about in novels, cruel death the material for so much poetry and art and yet no different than the blink of an eye or the clearing of a throat, for he was alive one moment and he simply wasn't the next. Jacov, irredeemably lost, no more than a lump of flesh, and perhaps, as his dear Buddhists believed, he would return, reincarnated, though how soon and as what animal who could say, and would I recognize his turbulent eyes in the eyes of a cow or a partridge or perceive his face in the face of a primate? And perhaps, as he'd always hoped, Jacov had joined his twin in the afterlife, running once more through the pastures of a land truer and more verdant than Knin's. No more genius resounding across my existence, no more life to give me life, no more hope to give me hope. An epoch had ended. Life would now be the dull, monotonous, never-ending gasp of a tired old man, each day an echo of the one before and a preface of the one to follow, and this would be my life if, by miracle, I even survived. And I recalled the most lucid description Jacov had ever given of melancholy: we were strolling through Stuttgart amid the dawning of his *gray period*, and turning the corner of Kriegsberg onto Ossletzky, Jacov explained that melancholy, in its purest form, was merely the realization of one's own insignificance, and the realization of this insignificance was, in itself, significant, and it was a placid feeling, melancholy was, a feeling of deepest joy hidden, embedded perhaps, inside the havoc of the human heart, and if one understood their own inherent sadness and didn't try to *defeat* it or *drown* it or *make it their foe* in a senseless and ceaseless battle, they might become, dare he say it, civilized and, with a little practice, even enlightened. It was the dead of winter, and the banks of snow, mute and colossal, towered beside us. I watched the clouds from Jacov's breath dissipate, and I wondered if the breath of another would be less potent since the thoughts others carried were inferior, because Jacov, in the torpor of his *gray period*, was turning poetic, explaining the significance of realizing one's own insignificance, and, turning the corner onto Wilhelmstraße, he explained that the depression and inertia that followed one's acceptance of their own insignificance was but an iota of the electromagnetic splendor of melancholy, a scrape along the hem of melancholy, a mere reflection of the cruddy backwater or pale suburb approaching the radiant city of melancholy. But you see, he added, this insignificance and the realization of this insignificance is wholly pure and honest and unpolluted by the world at large, and hence, in its own small way, is a feeling of such magnitude that one is forever marked. *That* is melancholy, he'd said, the ailment of artists and visionaries alike, and yes, he said, it hollows a person out, and yes, he said, it is slow and tedious and often feels common, but the humbling that follows is nothing short of miraculous, for if the world were a sadder and more reflective place and people looked inward instead of outward, can you not admit that the world would improve? And Jacov went on to say that melancholy was no less than the salvation of the world, a humbling at the feet of mortality, and the small glimpse he'd been given when his dear twin had died was what he'd been searching for ever since. To have the sliver of a feeling, he'd said, the flash of a higher light, he'd said, only to see it vanish, well of course I went after it, and I've spent my life going after it. And I held Jacov's head in my hands, kissed his brow, and cried, who can say for how long, and if an arrow had pierced my heart it would've been more mournful and true than if I'd survived, though this didn't happen, and the night was sober and silent, and with the *Origin Books* now in my possession I left him in the field, irretrievably lost, and in a stupor I returned to the forest, and it could have been a day or a week but time passed, for at one moment it was night and at another it was day, and however long I slept I finally awoke to the wizened face of an old man gazing at me with the inquisitiveness of a child, and I felt a tremor of recognition for it was Emiliano Gomez Carrasquilla! At least he resembled the mosaics and portraits Jacov had appointed across the salons and corridors of the second Stuttgart castle, an image inspired by the sole photograph Jacov had ever come across, a grainy photo on the back of his book-length essay *Energy of Joy*, inverted by Jacov as *Fatigue of Misery*; he was older, of course, but the brown, bottomless eyes and full lips of my master's great sage couldn't be mistaken for anyone else, although this man's eyes, at least up close, appeared to be green or at least hazel, but no matter, it had to be Carrasquilla, for who else would be tramping these woods all alone? Carrasquilla was stooped, as if walking were a great trial, and there was a crazed, manic expression in his eyes; twigs and bits of leaves were entangled in his beard; he held a walking stick in one hand and a burlap sack in the other. Adorned in a withered robe and a pair of decrepit sandals, he seemed not the least perturbed to come upon a white man asleep against the base of a tree. I gestured with open palms to indicate peaceful intentions, but Carrasquilla was beyond all of this, indifferent to the threats of an earthly death, for in his wisdom he was unmistakably free, and my gesture likely appeared to him primitive and ignoble. He shook the burlap sack, making a metallic noise, and motioned for me to follow. I stood and accompanied this frail creature, and we walked for less than a minute to a small clearing in the trees where Carrasquilla had set up camp, merely a fire with a few large stones arranged as a sort of minor fortress, all of it surrounded by thick prodigious trees. With paint or chalk, words and symbols had been inscribed on the stones, though the language appeared to be of his own invention, strange shapes and patterns that appeared to spell out some indecipherable message, a code of either prophecy or lunacy. Carrasquilla sat on a stone and unpacked his sack, smiled a toothless smile, café, he muttered as explanation, setting up a small tin pot and boiling water for coffee. Carrasquilla? I man-aged, and this strange old man, who resembled Carrasquilla so long as Carrasquilla's eyes were a different color, who surely *was* Carrasquilla if Carrasquilla had lived to be no less than a hundred years old and perhaps a little older, this man who undoubtedly *had* to be Carrasquilla, answered by showing me his gums, tengo familia en estos árboles, he muttered, estos árboles susurran sabios consejos, and then he laughed the sweetest, most innocent laugh I'd ever heard, although, to be honest, it also sounded like the gravest and most vulgar laugh I had ever heard, a little bit deranged too, but I forgave him, for without Carrasquilla there would be no Jacov, and without Jacov, who exactly was I? I forgave him his lunacy too, for soli-tude leaves its mark on a man as I myself had borne witness to; alone for a day, two at most, and already I was sensing the cal-loused knuckles of mania rapping on my door. This man, who was surely Carrasquilla if Carrasquilla had somehow grown hair where he had been bald before and was perhaps a foot and a half taller than what Jacov had believed, wasn't just old; he appeared to have eclipsed age itself, the point when a man passes certain trials and reemerges stronger and more vibrant, as though both time and age have been momentarily defeated, and in the translucence of his aged flesh and the abundance of his green eyes I knew all of this would dissolve, for looking at this man somehow gave me faith. In his demented eyes, among the stench of his robe, I once again considered living. Thanks to the company of another person, my faith in life was restored. I would endure. Somehow I would find civilization, and I pictured myself heaving once more across the Atlantic with the *Origin Books* pressed against my stomach, the *Origin Books* containing a future replete with deciphering and sharing Jacov's vision, and thus, a Europe of the new century where anything was possible, where men and women would come to know compassion and understanding and empathy through the world-weariness of melancholy, those somber Viennese melancholies and opulent Hungarian melancholies and those harsh and foreboding German melancholies, not to mention those austere Jewish melancholies, all of which Europe would embrace in the immensity of its heart, for melancholy was the emotion of compassion and reflection, melancholy simply containing the best inside ourselves, and I envisioned a century of peace and understanding in Europe, galvanized by Jacov's writings, holder of the highest and most immaculate Croatian melancholy to ever exist, for once the code was broken or decrypted or unraveled, in short, once the *Origin Books* had been translated, the knowledge of his life's work would spill, cascading, across the land. Jacov would be resurrected, and I felt the twentieth century welling up inside me, a century that promised to be more placid and untroubled than any in history, and if I heard the marching of boots, they were the boots of progress, and I envisioned a Europe with optimism and zeal and Jacov's death perhaps being the release I'd always needed and not known, and as I was handed the coffee, I felt the responsibility inherent in the *Origin Books*, for already they had begun to chafe my stomach, same as they had chafed my master's. Poor Jacov, not alive to see the century he would shape, and as I sipped the coffee, more bitter and better than any I'd ever had, I relished the future as one relishes the hope that lingers after a happy dream. Europe and the twentieth century and Jacov's masterpiece raised high inside the bookstores of the great continent, and perhaps Sonja would help translate the English editions, and why not? And all of this seemed true and good and made me infinitely content, and I considered in which direction Montevideo lay, and perhaps Carrasquilla had a compass or the ability to assist? Yet when asked he merely mumbled words that sounded vaguely Spanish but could've just as easily been Portuguese or perhaps gibberish, and he threw some sticks onto the fire. He crossed his legs and began to hum, and slowly he rocked back and forth, and without knowing why or when, I had joined him, in the humming, that is, and as we hummed the old sage smiled to himself, a knowing smile, a sagacious smile, a smile of benevolence and peace that conjured the cosmos, and somehow I knew I would survive, and the world itself would advance, and neither one of us would ever face a sad day again for the rest of our lives.

An immense and eternal thank you to Chris Fischbach, who believed in me and gave my book life.

Thank you, Chris Cander, who pushed me when it mattered.

Thank you: Carla Valadez, Daley Farr, Nica Carrillo, Lizzie Davis, Zeena Yasmine Fuleihan, Annemarie Eayrs, Timothy Otte, and everyone else at Coffee House—you're all amazing.

No book is written by itself, and I'm ever thankful for the generous reading and guidance of my editors, Carla Valadez and Anitra Budd.

Thanks to my father, Richard, and stepmom, Jan, for your love and support in everything.

Thanks to my mom, Judy, for your love and support in everything.

Thanks to Erra Davis ("The Pea") for your unflagging love and encouragement.

Thank you to the first readers of the manuscript: Rodrigo Hasbún, Veronica Esposito, Keaton Patterson, Philip Boehm, Augusta Bartis (rest in peace), Sara Balabanlilar, Richard Haber, Mary Allen, Garreth Boresche, and Eduardo Cárdenas.

Thank you, David Cudar—a friend, poet, and mentor.

Thanks to Argonáutica Press.

Thank you, Pablo and Barbara Ruiz, for your friendship and support.

Thank you Efrén Ordóñez (my first translator), Daniel Peña, Taylor Davis-Van Atta, Philip Boehm, Marco Antonio Alcalá, Bryan Washington, Kent Wascom, Maureen McDole, Keaton Patterson, Ben Rybeck, Mandy Medley, Cameron Dezen Hammon, and Tobey Blanton Forney for your friendship and literary support.

Lastly, thank you Lina Murane, Lisa Dillman, Antonio Ruiz-Camacho, Heather Cleary, Sophie Hughes, Hernán Díaz, Caroline Casey, Bruno Ríos, and Danielle DuBois, who took the time to read my earlier work.

LITERATURE
is not the same thing as
PUBLISHING

Coffee House Press began as a small letterpress operation in 1972 and has grown into an internationally renowned non-profit publisher of literary fiction, essay, poetry, and other work that doesn't fit neatly into genre categories.

Coffee House is both a publisher and an arts organization. Through our *Books in Action* program and publications, we've become interdisciplinary collaborators and incubators for new work and audience experiences. Our vision for the future is one where a publisher is a catalyst and connector.

Funder Acknowledgments

Coffee House Press is an internationally renowned independent book publisher and arts nonprofit based in Minneapolis, MN; through its literary publications and *Books in Action* program, Coffee House acts as a catalyst and connector—between authors and readers, ideas and resources, creativity and community, inspiration and action.

Coffee House Press books are made possible through the generous support of grants and donations from corporations, state and federal grant programs, family foundations, and the many individuals who believe in the transformational power of literature. This activity is made possible by the voters of Minnesota through a Minnesota State Arts Board Operating Support grant, thanks to the legislative appropriation from the Arts and Cultural Heritage Fund. Coffee House also receives major operating support from the Amazon Literary Partnership, Jerome Foundation, McKnight Foundation, Target Foundation, and the National Endowment for the Arts (NEA). To find out more about how NEA grants impact individuals and communities, visit www.arts.gov.

Coffee House Press receives additional support from the Elmer L. & Eleanor J. Andersen Foundation; the David & Mary Anderson Family Foundation; Bookmobile; Dorsey & Whitney LLP; Foundation Technologies; Fredrikson & Byron, P.A.; the Fringe Foundation; Kenneth Koch Literary Estate; the Matching Grant Program Fund of the Minneapolis Foundation; Mr. Pancks' Fund in memory of Graham Kimpton; the Schwab Charitable Fund; Schwegman, Lundberg & Woessner, P.A.; the Silicon Valley Community Foundation; and the U.S. Bank Foundation.

The Publisher's Circle of Coffee House Press

Publisher's Circle members make significant contributions to Coffee House Press's annual giving campaign. Understanding that a strong financial base is necessary for the press to meet the challenges and opportunities that arise each year, this group plays a crucial part in the success of Coffee House's mission.

Recent Publisher's Circle members include many anonymous donors, Suzanne Allen, Patricia A. Beithon, the E. Thomas Binger & Rebecca Rand Fund of the Minneapolis Foundation, Andrew Brantingham, Robert & Gail Buuck, Dave & Kelli Cloutier, Louise Copeland, Jane Dalrymple-Hollo & Stephen Parlato, Mary Ebert & Paul Stembler, Kaywin Feldman & Jim Lutz, Chris Fischbach & Katie Dublinski, Sally French, Jocelyn Hale & Glenn Miller, the Rehael Fund-Roger Hale/Nor Hall of the Minneapolis Foundation, Randy Hartten & Ron Lotz, Dylan Hicks & Nina Hale, William Hardacker, Randall Heath, Jeffrey Hom, Carl & Heidi Horsch, the Amy L. Hubbard & Geoffrey J. Kehoe Fund, Kenneth & Susan Kahn, Stephen & Isabel Keating, Julia Klein, the Kenneth Koch Literary Estate, Cinda Kornblum, Jennifer Kwon Dobbs & Stefan Liess, the Lambert Family Foundation, the Lenfestey Family Foundation, Joy Linsday Crow, Sarah Lutman & Rob Rudolph, the Carol & Aaron Mack Charitable Fund of the Minneapolis Foundation, George & Olga Mack, Joshua Mack & Ron Warren, Gillian McCain, Malcolm S. McDermid & Katie Windle, Mary & Malcolm McDermid, Sjur Midness & Briar Andresen, Maureen Millea Smith & Daniel Smith, Peter Nelson & Jennifer Swenson, Enrique & Jennifer Olivarez, Alan Polsky, Marc Porter & James Hennessy, Robin Preble, Alexis Scott, Ruth Stricker Dayton, Jeffrey Sugerman & Sarah Schultz, Nan G. & Stephen C. Swid, Kenneth Thorp in memory of Allan Kornblum & Rochelle Ratner, Patricia Tilton, Joanne Von Blon, Stu Wilson & Melissa Barker, Warren D. Woessner & Iris C. Freeman, and Margaret Wurtele.

For more information about the Publisher's Circle and other ways to support Coffee House Press books, authors, and activities, please visit www.coffeehousepress.org/pages/support or contact us at info@coffeehousepress.org.

Reinhardt's Garden was designed by
Bookmobile Design & Digital Publisher Services.
Text is set in Vendetta.